THE COWBOY'S LAST RODEO

LOUISE M. GOUGE

PLEASE RECYCLE
THIS PRODUCT IS RECYCLABLE

Recycling programs
for this product may
not exist in your area.

ISBN-13: 978-1-335-62171-9

The Cowboy's Last Rodeo

Love Inspired
22 Adelaide St. West, 41st Floor
Toronto, Ontario M5H 4E3, Canada
www.LoveInspired.com

HarperCollins Publishers
Macken House, 39/40 Mayor Street Upper,
Dublin 1, D01 C9W8, Ireland
www.HarperCollins.com

Printed in Lithuania

1 2 3 4 5 6 7 8 9 10 LIT 28 27 26 25

"That's Shadow over there…"

Raeder was already approaching the other stall, an undefinable expression on his face. "Hey, fella." He laid his forehead against the dark gray stallion's neck, and the horse nickered as it rubbed against him. "Sure have missed you." His voice held a plaintive note.

"Missed him?" June walked over to them. "How do you know Shadow? Dad bought him last fall… oh." She'd forgotten the horse had been among the possessions Raeder had to sell to pay for his hospital bill after his accident.

The fond yet rueful expression on his face almost broke her heart.

"It's good to see him so well taken care of."

"Looks like he's glad to see you, too. Raeder, you can ride him anytime."

Raeder had suffered more than a banged-up knee in last year's rodeo. He'd suffered the loss of a cowboy's best friend, a horse with whom he had a very special relationship. If she ever had to sell Sprinter, whom she'd raised from a newborn colt, she doubted she would ever recover from the loss.

Award-winning author **Louise M. Gouge** writes historical and contemporary fiction romances for Harlequin's Love Inspired imprint. She earned a BA in creative writing from the University of Central Florida and a Master of Liberal Studies degree from Rollins College. After teaching English and humanities for sixteen and a half years at Valencia College in Kissimmee, Florida, Louise now writes full-time. Contact Louise at louisemgougeauthor.blogspot.com, Facebook.com/louisemgougeauthor, and on X, @louisemgouge.

Books by Louise M. Gouge

Love Inspired

Safe Haven Ranch
Feuding with the Cowboy
The Cowboy's Last Rodeo

K-9 Companions

A Faithful Guardian

Love Inspired Historical

Finding Her Frontier Family
Finding Her Frontier Home

Four Stones Ranch

Cowboy to the Rescue
Cowboy Seeks a Bride
Cowgirl for Keeps
Cowgirl Under the Mistletoe
Cowboy Homecoming
Cowboy Lawman's Christmas Reunion

Visit the Author Profile page at LoveInspired.com for more titles.

Blessed be the God and Father of
our Lord Jesus Christ, who hath blessed us
with all spiritual blessings in heavenly places...
To the praise of the glory of His grace, wherein
He hath made us accepted in the Beloved.
—*Ephesians* 1: 3, 6

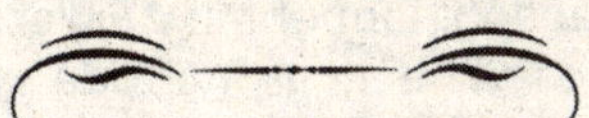

I fell in love with all things rodeo many years ago
while attending the Ski-Hi Stampede in Monte Vista,
Colorado. But I never would have written this story if
my beautiful granddaughter, Savannah Grace Reese,
hadn't been selected to be a rodeo queen—
Junior Miss Silver Spurs Rodeo in Kissimmee, Florida—
when she was thirteen. During Savannah's preparation
for that competition, former Miss Silver Spurs Rodeo
Lacie Stark coached her in all her rodeo queen secrets.
A true cattle-driving cowgirl, Lacie went on to become
Miss Rodeo Florida, an honor she truly deserved.
So I dedicate this story to the Ski-Hi Stampede,
the Silver Spurs Rodeo, Miss Lacie Stark, and of course,
my own Savannah Grace Reese.

Chapter One

"I'm sure your daddy will be here soon." June Mattson sat beside four-year-old Peanut in her Sunday school room, her arm around his slender shoulders, while he kept one thumb in his mouth and used his other hand to clutch a tiny, ragged, stuffed giraffe. His big brown eyes focused on her, he nodded, but a tiny wrinkle appeared on his smooth forehead.

Most Sundays, Peanut's dad was the first one to reach the preschool classroom at the end of the Sunday school hour. Where could he be? And why did he have to be late today? Her other students had been collected by their parents, and big church would start in ten minutes. She adored Peanut, but she really needed to get over to the sanctuary soon. Pastor Tim had asked her to give her testimony before the sermon, and she would need a minute or two to catch her breath after crossing the church campus.

"Hey, Miss June." Hat in one hand, Raeder Westfall clutched his cane in the other and limped through the door, giving her a big smile…a very attractive smile. "Hey, buddy." The handsome cowboy eased himself down on the nearby low wooden table and gathered his son into a gentle embrace. "Did you think I wasn't coming?" He tapped Peanut's nose. "Don't you worry. I'll always be here for you." He turned his attention to June. "Sorry for the delay, ma'am. Got caught up in a discussion with Miss Petra about chicken feed."

June nodded as though his explanation made sense. But it didn't. As Petra Murphy's ranch hand, surely Mr. Westfall and his boss had plenty of time to discuss such things outside of church.

"Time to go, Peanut." He struggled to stand with the help of his cane, inhaling sharply, and his face reddened as he regained his balance.

June bit her lip. Nothing offended a wounded, self-respecting cowboy more than some female offering to help him, as she'd learned when her brother, Eric, broke his back in a rodeo accident four years ago. "That's okay, Mr. Westfall—"

"You can call me Raeder, ma'am. That's pronounced *Ray*-der."

"Oh." She blinked. "Okay. Sure. Well, Raeder, Peanut and I were doing fine." Not really, but no need to discuss the child's fears in his presence. She gathered her Bible and hatbox. "When you get a minute, I'd like to tell you about something that happened today."

"You can go ahead and say it, ma'am." Raeder pulled Peanut into a side hug. "We don't keep secrets, do we, son?"

The adorable little boy, a tiny version of his handsome father, gazed up at him with a wistful expression and shook his head. "Tetha said she's lurgery to me."

Raeder seemed to smother a laugh. "Lurgery?" He gave June a questioning look.

Anxiety digging a pit in her stomach, June stifled the temptation to glance at her watch and laughed so he wouldn't notice her impatience. "Allergy. Tessa Simpson is allergic to peanuts." She took a step toward the door. "I'm sorry. I really need to get to church."

"Yeah. Sure." Frowning, he took Peanut's hand. "Come on, son. We gotta get to church, too." He stepped back to let June pass. "Thank you, Miss June."

She took another step, then stopped. "Maybe we can chat after the service." The words were out before she could stop them. She had a meeting with the stampede committee right after the service. As Miss Riverton Stampede, she didn't dare miss it. Everly Strait, the rodeo's Big Boss, didn't appreciate people arriving late, which might diminish her chances of getting some of her ideas on the agenda to help increase rodeo attendance. *Lord, please help me.*

"If it works out." Raeder didn't meet her gaze. "You go on, Miss June. We'll be there shortly."

Duty and compassion warred within her. She really wanted to help Peanut and his dad, but her promise to the pastor won out. Despite Raeder's obvious disappointment— or was it annoyance?—she gave them both a cheery smile. "Okay. See you later."

Leaving them to their slower pace, she sprinted across the wide lawn to the sanctuary's back door, right behind the choir as they filed into the choir loft. She slipped into a front pew in time to pull her Miss Riverton Stampede sash from her hatbox, along with her white hat, complete with its silver-and-gold queen crown fitted snuggly around the band, from its protective hatbox. She put them on, then took a quick look in her compact mirror, which revealed her makeup had made it through the Sunday school hour, with only a touchup needed for her lipstick. During the opening hymn, she managed to catch her breath and was prepared when Pastor Tim called her up to the podium, while the congregation applauded.

"Thank you so much. I'm so honored to be your Miss Riverton Stampede this year. On behalf of the stampede committee, I thank y'all for your support as we celebrate our ninety-third year of great Riverton rodeo this October. That's just five months from today! After church, please take a handful of these brochures—" she held up one of the trifold leaflets "—from the back tables to pass out to your friends and families. As you can see from the front picture, we're honored to have famous bull-riding champion Bret Hancock as a featured contestant, so be sure to mail out the brochures to folks out of town who love rodeos and our brave cowboys. We want this year's event to set a record for attendance."

She paused and prayed for her next words. "Y'all know we start every Sunday rodeo with Cowboy Church, which is really special to all our cowboys before they go out and compete in the arena. This year, our own Pastor Tim will be conducting the service." She slid a glance at the sixty-ish pastor. "We'll make a cowboy out of him yet." The pastor grinned and shrugged while the congregation chuckled.

"Cowboy Church is special to me, too," June continued, "because when I was ten years old, I trusted Jesus as my Savior at one of those services. I'm so grateful for my family of faith and so grateful for this church that supports my walk with Jesus. See y'all at the rodeo!" As always when she spoke about her faith or the rodeo, a feeling of exhilaration flooded her heart.

As she walked back to the pew, she noticed Raeder and Peanut sitting at the other end of the same row. Had they sat there because of her? Or because the sanctuary was packed today and this was the only pew left for latecomers? Peanut waved and grinned around the thumb in his mouth. Raeder barely glanced at her and certainly didn't offer her one of his all-too-attractive smiles. A pinch of annoyance replaced her elation. Was the cowboy still unhappy with her because she hadn't stayed to talk with him about Peanut? Or did he now realize why she'd had to hurry away and was embarrassed over their awkward moment at the Sunday school room door? *Or* was she being silly to expect this struggling single dad to give her the attention most cowboys gave her? *Well, Lord, there goes my pride again. Thinking only about myself.*

Besides, she wasn't looking for a relationship with a cowboy, especially not a rodeo cowboy. Four years ago, when her brother, Eric, became a paraplegic after a Brahman bull threw him off and trampled on his back, she promised herself she'd never marry or even date a rodeo cowboy. Ranching life was hard enough without a family man putting himself at risk like that. Surely, Raeder wouldn't compete again. Not after having his knee torn up so badly at last October's stampede. And surely not with a vulnerable little son who needed him. How could she impress that fact on him? It wasn't her place to confront him, but maybe she could gently persuade him that one of his responsibilities as a father was to stay as safe as possible so he could always be there for his precious little Peanut.

Now, if she could only figure out a way to talk to him beyond the few minutes before and after Sunday school in a way that didn't suggest she was chasing him…

Raeder didn't dare look down the pew at Miss June or he'd be in trouble. Between his involuntary reaction to her beauty—made even prettier by her rodeo-queen makeup and white hat with her crown around the hatband—and his embarrassment over delaying her walk to church, he had a feeling this crush was going to last longer than it should. Or than he wanted it to. He'd never been sweet on any lady besides Audra, his only love since childhood and the kindest, gentlest, most laid-back gal he'd ever known. They'd married right out of high school. When cancer took her life at twenty-two, only six months after Peanut was born, Raeder vowed he'd never love another woman. Then he enrolled Peanut in Miss June's Sunday school class. One look at her perfect face and her clear blue eyes, and he knew he'd have a problem reining in his heart.

What was he thinking? Miss June Mattson was a member of one of the largest, wealthiest ranching families in New Mexico. She'd never look twice at a broken-down cowboy like him. Besides, he simply had a crush based on her outward beauty. Well, that and her faith. And her sweet, gentle personality. Ugh! Why couldn't he stop these thoughts? One way would be to avoid her. At the end of the summer, Peanut would move up to the next Sunday school class, and Raeder could surely avoid Miss June in this large church.

Except that he needed to find out what happened in class today. Usually he sat in the back of the sanctuary, but by the time he and Peanut had gotten here, all those seats had been taken. Would Miss June think he was stalking her?

He needn't have worried. After the service, she seemed to have forgotten about talking to him. To be fair, she'd been surrounded by the usual bunch of cowboys, from sixteen to sixty, some even asking her to sign the rodeo brochures she handed them. She gave each one her sweet rodeo-queen smile and complied with their requests.

Raeder noticed Everly Strait was hovering impatiently nearby, along with several head honchos from the rodeo committee. A couple of them had spoken to him when he first arrived this morning, always checking on his healing progress and asking if he would miss riding in this fall's rodeo. They meant well, probably assuming he wanted pity, probably assuming he wouldn't or couldn't come back. They had no idea how much he longed to get back on those Brahman bulls—one in particular—so he could show himself *and* his son that no bull was going to permanently knock him out of the arena. Even though his surgeon warned that he shouldn't try to compete for at least another year, Raeder felt a strong need to satisfy that itch to compete if for no other reason than to rebuild his hard-won self-respect. He couldn't be finished with his career. Not yet. And he refused to admit he'd squandered it on a small-town rodeo.

Despite his strong work ethic, despite his earning a trade-school degree, despite his success at bull riding, his father continued to say he'd never amount to anything. If not for Pastor Tim's sermons about God loving every person right where they were, Raeder wouldn't bother to come to church. And he sure wouldn't follow in his old man's footsteps as a highly critical, uncaring father. Peanut would always know his love and support.

One of the committee ladies gave him a sympathetic nod and seemed about to come over and greet him, so he tucked his Bible under his arm, picked up his hat and cane and slowly wended his way up the aisle through crowds of chatting church members with Peanut at his side. No need to hurry. He'd be meeting up with Miss Petra to drive back to her ranch, and she always stuck around after services to visit with friends. His boss lady had promised her delicious meat loaf for lunch today, something Peanut ate without coaxing. Maybe that meat loaf and the ever-present cookies, along with Raeder helping him work on his chicken coop, would help his son forget whatever happened in class. Seeing Peanut happy always made for a great Sunday.

"Hold up, Raeder," Everly Strait called out and waved a hand at him. "We need to talk to you."

Surprise and curiosity halted Raeder in his tracks. Why in the world would they need to talk to him? Gripping Peanut's hand, he walked back down the sanctuary aisle to where Miss

June stood at the center of the six rodeo officials, looking like a rose among thorns. *Uh-oh. Gotta stop thoughts like that.*

Miss June gave him one of her beauty-queen smiles. Or maybe it was more like a cat-that-ate-the-cream smile. What in the world?

"Yessir, Mr. Strait. What can I do for you?"

"Good to see you up and about, Raeder." The fiftyish rancher stuck out a hand, which Raeder shook. "You know everybody here on the committee, so we don't need introductions, right? Listen, son, we got a situation, and Miss June just came up with a solution."

Raeder glanced at her dazzling smile, then looked back at Everly. "O-okay. How can I help?"

"Turns out ol' Bret Hancock's gone and got himself a brand-new career in television. Got an agent and everything." Everly chuckled. "Not sure he can act his way out of a paper bag, but he's signed to star in some new Western TV show. His gain, our loss. Turns out because we didn't have an actual contract with him, we can no longer use his image for our publicity due to some sort of legal thing those actors have. Like a copyright on their faces or something—"

Miss June interrupted Everly, and gave the man the closest thing to a look of annoyance her sweet face could muster. "But the good news is, we need a new famous cowboy for the publicity. Somebody top tier in the professional bull-riding association who can jump in right away and help us publicize the rodeo and attract lots of people. And here you are!"

Everly clapped Raeder on the shoulder. "What do you say? Will you help us out?"

His heart just about leaped out of his chest. His knees threatening to buckle, Raeder had to fight the urge to sit down. *Lord, is this from You? Do You want me to accept this job? I can't afford to quit working for Miss Petra...* But how could he accept without sounding desperate?

"Just so you know," Zeke Baldwin, another committee member said, "this is a paying gig." As a friend of Miss Petra and a frequent visitor to her ranch, Zeke couldn't help but be aware of Raeder's financial situation. Yet he added, "Not that you need to worry about such things."

Raeder sent him a grateful nod. "Man, sounds like a lot of work." He looked down at Peanut. "What do you think, son? Should we help promote the rodeo?"

Peanut's brown eyes brightened. "Me, too?"

Raeder slid a glance at Everly to check his reaction. If he couldn't take Peanut with him, he'd have to decline. But a sudden longing flooded his chest. Accepting meant he didn't have to sit on the sidelines. Didn't have to deal with the pitying looks from his fellow cowboys every time he ran into one. To his relief, Everly gave a quick nod.

"No reason why not. That'll remind everybody that rodeos are a family event."

Raeder laughed to try to disguise the relief filling him. "Well, then. I guess me and Peanut and—" he nodded toward the rodeo queen "—Miss June are gonna publicize ourselves a rodeo." She looked mighty pleased with herself, but not in a stuck-up way. He sure did owe her a debt of gratitude for putting his name forward, even though it was probably just because he was handy, and they were in a pinch.

"Do you mind signing a contract?" Everly asked.

"Everly!" Event coordinator Mrs. Austen shook her head. "A handshake is all we need."

"That's okay, ma'am." Raeder grinned at her. "Sounds like a handshake didn't seal the deal with Bret. I'll be happy to sign."

"That's fantastic!" Miss June clapped her hands like a kid

who'd just gotten a present from her grandma. "We already have a schedule, and I'll be so glad to have you along with me and my court. And, of course, Peanut, too." She gave Peanut a sweet smile, and the boy beamed back at her.

After some serious handshakes, backslapping and setting an appointment for signing the contract, Raeder gathered his stuff and his son and headed back up the sanctuary aisle. Time for some of Miss Petra's meat loaf.

Thank You, Lord, for giving me this chance.

Memories of his dad cut short his enthusiasm. What if he didn't succeed in bringing in the crowds the way Bret Hancock would have? What if he failed again? *Lord, please help me not to let these good folks down.*

June wasn't sure her suggestion had been the best idea. After all, she hoped and prayed Raeder wouldn't compete in bull riding again for the sake of his son. But the shock at learning Bret Hancock had backed out of the rodeo promotions caused her to focus on finding an immediate solution to the problem. The quickest one was right in front of them all—Raeder Westfall. The enthusiasm of the committee members when they took her suggestion encouraged her momentarily, because she sure didn't want to be the last Miss Riverton Stampede if the rodeo failed and died away. That would be an embarrassment that would follow her all her life here in her hometown. Yet she couldn't help but have second thoughts about Raeder. What if his participation in the promotional tour encouraged him to return to a sport that had almost killed him? Then who would take care of Peanut?

"Miss June?" Jeff Sizemore, along with several other teens, awaited her a few rows away. "We going for pizza today?"

"Oh. Oh, yes, of course." June removed her hat and returned it to its hatbox, then slipped her sash over her head, rolled it and tucked it in beside her hat. "Let's get going."

She herded the group out the front door and assigned drivers and passengers to three vehicles. "See you all at Lorenzo's."

Second only to teaching her preschool kids in Sunday school, her favorite ministry was her weekly after-service trips for pizza with the church's teens. These outings helped to draw in kids like Jeff, who'd been an outsider, and let them know they were loved and accepted. June's cousins, twins Bobby and Mandy Mattson, were especially good at welcoming newcomers, such as their new stepsister, Zoey. A sweet girl with cerebral palsy, she could have easily been ignored by other kids, but Bobby and Mandy had befriended her from the moment they met her when she enrolled in high school last fall.

As June climbed into her own Chevy pickup, she saw Raeder standing beside his Bronco with Peanut. He looked her way and touched the brim of his hat. Giving him a big wave and a smile, she felt a warm tug on her heart. No, she hadn't made a mistake. Raeder would be a much better partner in her promotional efforts. Bret was nice enough, but he was the only cowboy she'd ever known who checked his appearance in every mirror he passed. Sure, he could ride those bulls, but June doubted he'd ever been a true cowboy, as in actually working with cattle on a ranch. Raeder was the real deal, just like most of June's relatives. For that alone… well, and also for being a good father to Peanut, she could respect him. Now, if she could just persuade him, gently, of course, to stay safe for Peanut and start calling his son by his Christian name, whatever that might be, she could call her work for them well done.

* * *

Standing beside his ride in the church parking lot, Raeder watched as Peanut ran to Miss Petra for a hug like he hadn't seen her for a week, instead of all of them riding together for church just three hours ago. The slender, middle-aged lady with red-blond hair treated Peanut with the same kindly affection she generously gave her granddaughter, Sassy. The ten-year-old girl was like a big sister to Peanut, who followed her around Miss Petra's small ranch like a puppy. When Raeder was in the hospital after his accident, Miss Petra showed up one day and petitioned the court to take care of Peanut. Then she'd hired Raeder as her ranch hand, although it took him months to work up to the harder chores. Still, he liked to think his work helped the single lady as much as she helped him, but if both sides were weighed on a scale, he was pretty sure she'd win.

They climbed into Raeder's two-year-old Ford Bronco, the last remnant of better days when he could buy whatever he and Peanut needed, and they drove out of the church parking lot toward her ranch. Before his accident, he'd built up a pretty good nest egg toward buying his own ranch one day through his frequent rodeo winnings.

Raeder had participated in rodeos since he turned sixteen, and he'd earned the right to join the Professional Rodeo Cowboys Association and participate in the Professional Bull Riders league, which meant he could purchase health insurance through those organizations. But his many medical bills and physical therapy had cost a lot of money beyond the insurance coverage. That left his nest egg with a balance barely above zero and this paid-for Bronco. If not for Miss Petra hiring him and giving him and Peanut a home in her old bunkhouse, he and his son would be homeless, not to mention he may have had to sell the SUV like he'd had to sell his beloved horse, Shadow. If not for Miss Petra insisting on their going to church with her, he wouldn't have returned to his faith in the Lord, either. Maybe it wasn't the life he'd envisioned when he started riding professionally, but he was grateful for it.

With their lives pretty much intertwined, he was quick to share his news about joining the rodeo's promotions as they drove toward the ranch. "I'll be sure to get my work done for you, Miss Petra. That'll always come first."

"Now, don't you be worrying about that, Raeder." She shook her head. "I'm happy they're showing you the respect you deserve." She chuckled. "And, of course, it won't hurt any for you to spend some time with that sweet June Mattson."

Feeling heat rise up his neck, he shot her a look. "I should add that Zeke Baldwin put in a good word for me at the meeting, so maybe I should return the favor. Didn't you say you'd let him take you to dinner if he started coming to church? Well, he was there—"

"Say, Peanut." She glanced over her shoulder. "Did you have a nice Sunday school?"

"Tetha said she's lurgery to me."

Raeder glanced in the special mirror attached below his rearview mirror that allowed him to check on his son in the back seat as he drove. Peanut gave Miss Petra the same vulnerable look he'd given Raeder in the Sunday school room.

Miss Petra questioned Raeder with one raised eyebrow, but she caught on quicker than he had. "She said she's allergic to you?" She chuckled in her deep, throaty way. "Why, honey, when a little girl says something like that, it means she's sweet on you."

Peanut jerked his gaze toward Raeder's reflection in the little mirror, then looked back at Miss Petra. "Like sugar?"

She laughed again. "Yes, indeed, honeypot. You're sweet as sugar."

Peanut grinned, all vulnerability gone.

Count on this kind lady to turn hurt feelings into a smile. Just like Miss June did.

Now, why was he thinking about her again? Before he could examine his useless musings, his cell phone sounded with its *moooo* ringtone that always made Peanut giggle. The number flashing on the screen wasn't familiar, but he punched the connect button on his dash, anyway.

"Raeder?" The unmistakable voice of Miss June sounded through the truck's speakers.

He swallowed hard, barely noticing the chuckle coming from Miss Petra in the passenger seat. "Yes, ma'am?"

"Hey, Raeder, it's June Mattson."

"Yes, ma'am. What can I do for you?" He could hear muted background chatter and guessed she was still driving with her truckload of teenagers.

"Do you mind if I come out to see you this afternoon to talk about our promotional tour and some other stuff? That is, if you don't think Miss Petra will mind?"

"I don't mind." Miss Petra laughed again as she reached across the console and nudged Raeder's shoulder.

Raeder shot her a panicked look and shook his head. The last thing he needed was his boss lady playing matchmaker for him, as she had for her own daughter this past spring. Miss Juliet would be marrying Sam Mattson in a few weeks, and she'd asked Peanut to be their ring bearer.

"Sure, Miss June." A car horn sounded behind him, so Raeder forced his focus on the highway traffic. Too many wrecks happened on these roads when drivers got distracted.

"Great. See you around three, okay?"

"Sure. Okay." Raeder swallowed hard again. Then laughed

inwardly at his foolishness. She wasn't coming to see him, she was coming to see her promotional-tour partner. And that "other stuff" was probably about Peanut. Like any good teacher, she probably thought his son needed extra help. He'd have to set her straight on that.

Over the next two hours, he kept reminding himself to keep everything in a sensible perspective. This meeting wasn't about him or Miss June. It was about the rodeo. Surely, given enough time working with her, his involuntary reactions to her beauty would mellow, and he would be able to talk to her without his heart hiccupping.

As soon as he and Peanut finished lunch with Miss Petra in her ranch house, he put his son down for a nap in their bunkhouse. Although he didn't own this humble, hundred-year-old structure, he'd made it a cozy home for Peanut. This being a nice day, he'd invite Miss June to sit outside with him so his son couldn't hear their conversation, in case she wanted to bring up the other kids teasing him about his name.

Raeder made sun tea in a gallon milk jug, then set out quart canning jars to drink from, along with a sugar bowl and some lemon slices. Made sure there was plenty of ice in the old fridge's metal ice trays. Fretted because he hadn't thought to ask Miss Petra for some of those chocolate-chip cookies… then felt heat rise up his neck when the lady brought a plateful of them out to him.

"Here's some more cookies for, ahem, Peanut. Wink, wink."

"Thank you, ma'am." Raeder's face heated up some more. "I believe you were gonna work on that quilt for Miss Juliet's wedding gift this afternoon, weren't you?"

She snickered. "Don't worry, hon. I'm not gonna intrude on your visit with June." She started to leave, then turned back. "And I'll try real hard not to peek out the window when she arrives." She walked away laughing.

But to Raeder, it was no laughing matter. He would not be one of those pathetic men who reached higher than they should, or one of those slick types who tried to charm their way into a good lady's graces. If the Lord wanted him to remarry, wanted Peanut to have a new mama, He'd have to bring a less famous and certainly less wealthy woman across his path.

Miss June arrived promptly at three and parked her pickup near the bunkhouse fence. She'd changed from her pretty white Sunday dress into well-worn jeans, Western boots and a blue T-shirt. Her blue eyes caught the shirt color and looked all the more appealing.

Stop that! Her fairly new vehicle was just another sign she was way out of his league.

"Hey, Miss June." He walked over to greet her. "Shall we sit there in the shade." He indicated the two wooden chairs under the cottonwood tree.

"Sure. This is such a nice peaceful spot." She noticed the refreshments. "Oh, you didn't have to do this."

He coughed away the strain in his throat. "It ain't much. And I thought we should visit away from the house so Peanut won't wake up and barge in on our talk."

"Of course. Good idea." She sat and accepted the tea he offered, adding lemon and a half teaspoon of sugar. "Thanks. And I'm so glad you mentioned Peanut. Do you mind me asking why you call him that?"

Raeder sat back. He should turn the conversation to the rodeo, but courtesy required him to answer her question. "It's the nickname his mama gave him."

"Oh." Her voice and expression turned all sympathetic.

He didn't want to deal with her pity. "It's not like cowboys don't have all sorts of nicknames. Skeeter. Bucky. Spike. Tex. Slim. Dusty. Rusty." Or what his father called him. Loser. No, he'd best not go there. "Now, about the rodeo—"

"But have you ever considered how a nickname like Peanut can cause a child to form a negative opinion of himself? Oh, not like Tessa's teasing. Actually, he was worried that he might accidentally hurt her." She smiled in an almost maternal way. "Such a kindhearted little boy to think of her instead of himself. So what's his given name?"

Where was she going with this? "Raeder. Junior."

There went that smile again. "Aw. That's sweet. And very unusual. Where on earth did you get a name like *Rae*der?" She leaned toward him, and her smile turned impish. "Are you a Viking?"

He chuckled, appreciating her lighter tone. "Don't know 'bout that. Maybe. But my mama always liked opera, and one day when she was a kid, she went to a concert where a baritone named Raeder Anderson sang. She liked that name and held on to it in the back of her mind. When she married my pa and then I came along, she told him that would be my name. Maybe she hoped I'd sing like my namesake." He laughed again. "But I sure don't sing opera. Don't even like it."

"What kind of music do you like?"

"Well, duh, Miss Rodeo. What else but country and western?" Oops. Had he made a mistake to tease her?

From her musical laughter, he could see he hadn't.

"But seriously, Raeder, I'm concerned about Peanut's self-esteem. Did any of his preschool classmates tease him about his name?"

Raeder shifted in his chair. "He didn't go to preschool."

Now, she stared at him like a cross schoolmarm. "Why on earth not? Preschool is so important for rural and ranch kids. Living away from typical neighborhoods where they can easily meet other children, how will they learn to socialize with their peers?" She took a sip of her tea before going on. "Well, I'm sure he'll catch up when he attends kindergarten this fall."

My, my, she was getting nosy. "He ain't…isn't going to kindergarten. I'm homeschooling him." Better use proper grammar so she couldn't claim he wasn't qualified to teach his own son.

"Hmm." She peered at him over the top of her quart jar of tea. "Not to intrude, Raeder…"

Too late for that.

"…but aren't you a bit busy running this ranch to give him the attention he needs?"

Raeder stared off across the alfalfa field that would soon be ready for its first cutting of the year. "My son works alongside me, whatever I'm doing. Unless it's dangerous. Then Miss Petra watches him like she promised the social worker when she asked permission to help us out."

Miss June's blue eyes narrowed, and her lips quirked to one side. "Aren't you concerned he won't learn all the subjects he needs to be well educated?"

"It's the way I was raised. If it was good enough for me, it's good enough for my son. And so is my trade-school education, which makes me qualified to maintain the machinery around here, something every ranch needs." He waved a hand to take in the nearby aged tractor and combine, then huffed out a frustrated breath. This talk wasn't going well at all, except to show him another side to a lady he'd thought almost perfect. "How many kids have you raised, Miss June?" He couldn't keep the annoyance from his tone.

Her eyes widened briefly, then her expression softened. "First of all, just call me June. I'm not your great aunt." She laughed softly, then grew serious again. "I'm not a parent, but I do know about children. My minor is in childhood psychology, and I've worked with preschoolers in Sunday school since I was twelve, plus I have too many younger cousins to count, so I do know what children need."

"Uh-huh." Raeder took a long drink of his tea, then set his jar on the table. "Well, *June*, I don't mean to be rude, but don't you think we should talk about the rodeo promotions? I don't have the first idea of exactly what I'm supposed to do."

"Oh." She blinked those blue eyes. "Yes, of course. I brought the schedule." She pulled a folded paper from her jeans pocket and handed it to him. "As you can see, we have a list of rodeos to visit this summer, along with a bunch of local and state businesses to assure their sponsorship. We'll meet with the committee tomorrow afternoon for more details, and Tuesday, we'll have our first publicity photo shoot." She studied him up and down with a critical eye. "We might have to spruce you up a bit, if you don't mind."

He snorted out a laugh. "Spruce me up?"

She laughed…again. "Sorry. Just that we need you to look picture-perfect. Hey, listen, we rodeo queens have to go through all sorts of stuff to look perfect. Makeup, hair extensions, clothes selections, matching boots and hats." She smirked. "I promise we won't be too hard on you."

His heart sank. "Oh, man. What've I got myself into?" He ran a hand through his hair, which could probably use a trim about now.

"Oh, don't worry. It'll be fun."

"Oh, sure." He rolled his eyes, then stood. "Listen, I apologize, but I gotta get Peanut up from his nap so we can tend to his chickens. You want to stick around?" He hadn't meant to ask her that, but the words just came out.

"Aw, that'd sure be fun, but I'd better go. I got my own

chores to do at my folks' ranch before evening church." She got up and walked toward her truck, waving over her shoulder. "See you tomorrow."

As she drove away, Peanut came running from the house. "Daddy, where's Miss June going?" Close to tears, he stared after her car.

"She had to get home to do chores, just like we do." Raeder picked him up and gave him a gentle hug. "Don't worry, partner. You'll see her again tomorrow when we start working on rodeo stuff."

His little face broke into a wide grin. "You'll see her, too?"

Had Peanut picked up on his attraction to the lady? He'd have to be more careful in the coming days. "Sure will."

Not that Raeder looked forward to being "spruced up." But what could he do? He'd promised to promote the rodeo, whatever it took. Contract or not, he'd never been one to go back on his word, and he wasn't about to start now.

Chapter Two

As June drove away from the Murphy Ranch, her mind exploded with ideas for giving Raeder a makeover. As ruggedly handsome as he was with his slightly scruffy appearance, she knew the older folks on the committee—especially Alice Austen—would prefer a more clean-cut look. Happily, he hadn't squawked too much at her suggestion about the photo shoot. Forget feeling sorry for him because of his lost rodeo career. Like Bret Hancock, he might just have a new career, only his would be as a cowboy model.

She was glad he hadn't brought up competing in the bull riding. As the single father of a vulnerable little boy, he'd had no business in the first place engaging in something that could have gotten him killed. Surely, his injury proved that to him. At least only his one knee was shattered, and his concussion hadn't been as bad as the docs first suspected. The men in her family often competed in rodeos, but once they married and had children, they had the good sense to retire from the more dangerous events, or to at least take up the less-dangerous ones, like steer wrestling or team roping. Life on the Mattson ranches was dangerous enough without inviting more injuries, like her brother had.

If only Eric's injury had been as simple as Raeder's. Even today, her brother had to miss church because of health complications, which meant Mom had to stay home, too. With her thriving small animal veterinary clinic and Dad's equally thriving large animal, vet-and-farrier business, they sometimes required June's help with Eric. She never minded being there for her older brother, who'd always been there for her. But when she was crowned Miss Riverton Stampede and took on the accompanying responsibilities, they'd had to hire someone outside the family to take care of him—the man who'd always taken care of everybody else. At six foot three, he'd held his own alongside the best of the other Mattson men in height, character and faith…until that horrible bull ride.

Despite the family's needs, they'd all encouraged June to make a run for the title, especially Eric. Most local girls with queen ambitions entered the competition starting at six for Little Miss and thirteen for Junior Miss, with sixteen being the youngest entrants for the top title. It had taken June until she turned twenty-one to decide she wanted to join the ranks of several other Mattson women who'd competed for the crown. She'd never considered herself all that special, but the title brought with it much more male attention than she'd ever wanted. Once her year of serving ended, she had no intention of going to the next level and entering the Miss Rodeo New Mexico pageant.

In traveling around the state with other New Mexico rodeo queens, she'd seen how a girl could get used to all that attention and have her head turned in the wrong direction by some cute but egotistical cowboy, or even a rich, older sponsor. But June couldn't wait to get back to working with her folks at their vet clinics and being available to help with Eric, along with teaching her precious preschool kids in Sunday school. If she still had time for barrel racing with her registered quarter horse, Sprinter, in the local rodeos, that would be great, too.

As she headed home to their small property outside of Riverton, Raeder Westfall's handsome face edged back into her mind. She'd noticed as they sang hymns in the church service this morning what a fine baritone voice he had. Maybe he should have taken up the same career as the man he'd been named for. She laughed. Well, maybe not opera. But how about the country music he liked? Add that to a cowboy modeling career, and he'd be sure to find success. Too bad she hadn't taken the chance to suggest all of her bright ideas before they both needed to get busy with chores. How could she steer him away from bull riding so he didn't end up like Eric…or worse? How could she get him interested in something else, like modeling or music?

"I know," she answered herself out loud. "I'll tell Wayne he should invite Raeder to sing in the church choir. He's always saying he needs more men." And that should put a bow on her attempt to tell Raeder how to run his life.

Poor man. He sure was miffed at her for saying Peanut should be in kindergarten this fall. But she truly believed the darling little boy would benefit from being in one of Riverton's fine grade schools. Now, whom should she speak to about convincing him this was the best plan for his son?

So much for putting that bow on her thoughts. Why couldn't she keep from thinking about that man? She couldn't possibly consider a relationship with him. Or anyone else until next spring. Part of being Miss Riverton Stampede meant she had to remain single or forfeit her crown. Besides that, the man she married would likely be someone she could work alongside, maybe an equine vet like Dad, or a big rancher like her cousin Rob, or a lawyer like cousins Sam and Will. Since childhood, she'd assumed the Lord would bring her the right man at the right time. Would she truly be open to His will, or would she have a checklist that suited her own wishes and wants? Best to stay busy with her family and rodeo responsibilities and let the Lord guide her path.

After arriving at their three-hundred-acre spread, three miles from Riverton, she parked in the garage and made her way into the kitchen, where the aroma of Mom's herb-laced sourdough bread filled the room.

"Mission accomplished?"

When June had come home from her pizza outing with the teens, Mom had listened to June's concerns about Peanut and her thoughts about tweaking Raeder's appearance for the photo shoot.

"More or less." June helped herself to a slice of the fresh baked bread and applied butter as she gave a brief report on her visit, and added, "Raeder wasn't excited about the idea of a makeover."

Mom laughed. "Not many men would be."

"I suppose not. I may need one of the guys on the committee to encourage him."

"Hey, sweetheart." Dad wandered into the room. "Were you just out at Petra Murphy's ranch?" He accepted the slice of bread Mom handed him.

Her mouth full, June nodded.

"Did you happen to take a look at her old gelding?"

June glanced at Mom. "Uh, no. Was I supposed to?"

"I just thought she might have mentioned Darby. That's okay. If she didn't say anything to you, it's not an emergency. She caught me after church and asked me to come check on him, so I'll go tomorrow. Want to come along?"

June traded another look with Mom. If she went out to Miss Petra's place so soon, would Raeder think she was being a pest? Besides, she'd see him tomorrow afternoon at the rodeo planning committee meeting.

"Come on, honey." Dad chuckled. "It'll be a good experience for you. One of these days you'll have to decide whether to follow your mom or me in your veterinary career path."

"Yeah, well, about that," she replied. "I may decide to switch my career choice. You know how much I love working with children. Maybe I'll go into early childhood education." Not that she was serious about such a change…

"I won't object to that, but I do think you should explore all your options." Dad poured himself a cup of coffee and sat at the kitchen table. "Even if you decide to change your focus, go with me tomorrow. For cases like this, I always take my assistant, but you know Ryan's wife just had their first baby, so he needs to take the week off to help out at home."

"I can do without you at the clinic," Mom said to her. "Go on and help your father."

"Mom…" She really didn't want Raeder to get the wrong idea.

"Come on, June. I really could use your help."

Once Dad's mind was made up, June knew better than to argue. "Yessir."

Maybe it wasn't such a bad idea after all. She'd get to see Peanut, *and* maybe she'd try calling him by his given name… or maybe just his initials, RJ, to see how he liked it. Surely Raeder would see what a good idea it was.

"From what I could find out when I took him in, he's close to twenty-three years old, if not older." Miss Petra stood beside Darby's head and held his halter while Doc Mattson checked over the old quarter horse gelding. "We rescued him last year because it don't seem right to put down a critter with such intelligent eyes." She ran a hand down the horse's long head, and he leaned in for more. "Don't know what's going on with him now."

Raeder stood outside the stall with Peanut riding on his

shoulders as they watched the vet examine Darby and take a listen to his chest and belly with a stethoscope. Raeder had been around quarter horses all his life, and he agreed with his boss. The gelding had warm, wise eyes and a gentle disposition, plus he was "bomb-proof," never startling at sudden noises. Which made him the perfect horse for kids to learn how to ride on. He'd already put Peanut on him several times with good results. Darby seemed to enjoy it as much as Peanut because he didn't have to be coaxed to come in from the pasture. One look at Peanut climbing the fence rail, and he trotted over to greet him. Raeder was hoping he could give lessons and earn a little money on the side, if Miss Petra didn't mind.

On the far side of the fifteen-hands horse, the top of June's baseball cap was barely visible. When she and her dad arrived, she seemed to avoid Raeder's gaze. He didn't have to guess why. When they finished their talk yesterday, he'd practically dismissed her, not exactly gentlemanly behavior. He'd have to figure out a way to apologize, maybe when they met up later today for the committee meeting.

Not that he minded her coming out here. It was kind of cute the way she tagged along with her veterinarian father like she was on a take-your-kid-to-work day. And he appreciated the way she was so comfortable around Darby and how she petted the barn cats that wound around her boots and yowled for attention and treats.

"Welp." Doc unplugged his stethoscope from his ears and put it in his black bag. "His heart and intestines sound good. All I can say is it's old age slowing him down. These old cow ponies do a lot of hard work in their years of service, and it tends to wear down their joints." He grinned at Miss Petra. "Just like us humans." He patted Darby's rump. "I think he has plenty more good years in him for teaching kids to ride, so I'll prescribe a monthly dose of Adequan for his arthritis and see if that perks him up a bit. You want chewable or injectable?" He glanced at Raeder before turning to Miss Petra.

"Um, well…" Miss Petra's forehead wrinkled. "Now, how much is that gonna cost?"

"Injectable." Raeder would do without new jeans and whatever else he needed for the rodeo tour so he could pay for the expensive medication. He couldn't bear to see a good old cow pony suffer pain any more than he could let his son fall sick without doing all he could to get him well.

"Now, Raeder—"

"Now, Miss Petra." He gave her his most charming grin, the one Audra used to love. "We'll manage. Maybe ol' Zeke'll come out again this week and buy some hay. That'll help. Doc, can I come over to your place and pick that Adequan up today after my meeting?"

"No need for that." Doc finished packing up the tools of his trade. "June can bring it to you at your meeting this afternoon."

The party in question glared at her dad for a quick second. "Sure. I can do that." Then she gave Raeder her Sunday-school-teacher smile. Maybe she wasn't put out with him after all. "Why don't I take Peanut into town for a hamburger and ice cream, and meet up with you at two o'clock?"

"Ice cream?" Peanut squealed. "Can I go, Daddy? Can I?"

Uh-oh. Now, she was talking about hamburgers and ice cream without asking Raeder's permission first. Didn't she know that to mention such treats was like making a promise? So much for her knowing about kids. Only one way to handle it.

"Well, now that you mention it, it's been a while since I took my son for a treat myself. So no need for you to bother." He'd have to raid Peanut's piggybank, but it would be worth it. Oh, my. Just being around this woman cost him money he couldn't afford to spend. Would he be making enough money doing the rodeo promo to make up for it?

"Oh." She blinked those big blue eyes, but not in a flirty way. More like disappointed. "Okay."

"Why don't you both go?" Miss Petra winked at Raeder. "And be sure to bring some ice cream back for Sassy. She likes cherry vanilla."

"Yes, ma'am." He knew better than to argue with his boss lady. And speaking of her granddaughter… "Say, why don't we just take Sassy with us, Peanut?" He didn't look at June for confirmation. "Y'all just head on back home, and I'll follow right behind you."

"Sounds good." Doc picked up his bag and ushered June out of the barn.

It didn't take long to collect Sassy, whose mama was glad to give permission. Since she and Miss Juliet moved to the ranch last year, Sassy had been like a big sister to Peanut and never minded the way he tagged along wherever she went. Earlier this year, they'd joined 4-H and started raising chickens together, which made Raeder proud. He wasn't quite so proud when the two kids went on an adventure that scared everybody real bad until the kids were found. Sassy had learned from that experience and had become much more responsible.

"Now, Peanut—" Sassy sat beside Peanut's booster chair in the back seat of Raeder's Bronco "—you know cherry vanilla is the best flavor, so you better be ordering that."

Not only was she sassy, but she was also bossy…kinda like her cousin, June Mattson. Maybe it ran in the family, at least in the females.

"I want spistachico." Peanut giggled in his cute way that always made Raeder's heart sing. He probably said he liked pistachio because it was fun to pronounce the word. Or, rather, mispronounce it.

Sassy giggled, too. "But it's gre-e-een…like veggies. Yuck!"

Their argument went back and forth, as usual, with lots more giggling and silly talk. Raeder wouldn't trade it for the world. He couldn't provide Peanut with a sibling, but the Lord had provided Sassy. He didn't know how Peanut would take it once Miss Juliet married Sassy's birth father, lawyer Sam Mattson, in a couple of weeks and they moved over to the Double Bar M Ranch. He'd have to keep his son even closer after that.

He parked in front of Doc Mattson's office, which was located on the small ranch where they lived, and let the kids out. Even for a short run into the building, he couldn't leave them alone in the vehicle.

Inside, Peanut ran to hug June, even though he'd seen her twenty minutes ago. "Miss June, I'm gonna get some *spistachico* ice cream."

"You are?" Clearly hiding a laugh, she hugged him back. "Sounds real yummy. And what flavor will you be having?"

For a second as he looked down at his son, Raeder thought she was asking him. Then he saw her focus was on Sassy.

"Cherry vanilla. Of course." Sassy rolled her eyes like it was a silly question. "You coming with us, Cousin June?" She'd caught on real quick to the way all the Mattsons addressed their relatives.

Now, June looked at Raeder. "Not this time."

"But next time," Sassy said firmly, not allowing for an argument to her plan.

"Maybe." June reached for the paper bag on the front desk and held it out to Raeder. "Here's your Adequan. If you need help giving Darby the shot—"

"Nope." Raeder all but snatched the bag from her, then felt heat rush up his neck as he handed her the cash payment. "Sorry. Not meaning to be rude, but I've been giving shots to horses since I was Sassy's age."

"Oh." She batted those eyes at him, again not in a flirty way. "Good to know. Same with me. Well, kids, y'all enjoy your ice cream. I've got work to do."

"But, Miss June," Peanut wailed, "why aren't you coming with us?"

"I'm so sorry, honey." She turned that sweet Sunday-school-teacher smile on his son. "I have a couple of things to do for my dad before I head out for the rodeo committee meeting."

If not for the gentle way she addressed his son, Raeder would have a hard time reminding himself she was way too bossy and way too far out of his league to claim his interest. Even so, every time she smiled like that, he felt like he'd been slammed in the chest. Mom always said, "Mind over feelings, son." While she'd meant it to help him deal with the rough way Pa always talked to him, the idea had also stood him in good stead when he needed to overcome his fear before riding bulls in a hundred different arenas around the country. Maybe he could apply the same principle when it came to this all-too-pretty woman. If not, he was only letting himself in for some serious heartbreak. And life had already given him enough of that through no fault of his own.

"Hold still." June gripped Raeder's chin the same way she would one of her fellow rodeo queens when applying makeup. Getting him ready for the photo shoot in her kitchen, she brushed powder over his well-formed cheeks and broad forehead. He'd fussed a little over having to give himself a close shave and fussed a lot over having to wear foundation to even out his unevenly sunburned complexion. Most cowboys had that line where their hats covered their foreheads and the lower part of their faces tanned. While it was a normal part of their appearance, it wouldn't make for good promo pics. "Hold still," she repeated when Raeder reached up to scratch his chin.

"Yes, ma'am." He blew out a long breath. "When y'all asked me to represent the rodeo, you forgot to mention all this girlie stuff I'd have to do. I don't know how you ladies manage it, but this'll be the last time I let anybody slather that goop all over my face. Couldn't they just photoshop the pictures if they want me to look all that pretty?" He grimaced as he said that last word.

June laughed. "Sure. They could. But it always looks fake. Now, quit talking so I can finish." She stood back and surveyed her work. "Perfect. Now, your hair."

He rolled his eyes. "If you must."

Actually, she liked the look of his untamed mass of blond curls, but it wouldn't do for a publicity picture because of the sharp contrast to her own carefully coiffed hair. She applied a dollop of mousse to her hands, rubbed them together, then gently ran the mousse through his hair, which she'd trimmed earlier. He'd stopped wincing at her touch, probably because he'd resigned himself to the inevitable. She'd had to deal with her own reticence at grooming the handsome cowboy, but she often styled her brother's hair, so that helped her get past her discomfort. After a few minutes of using her curling iron to tame his curls as best she could, she combed it into a picture-perfect style and spritzed it with hairspray. Then she stood back and surveyed her work.

"Perfect." She removed the nylon salon cape from around his shoulders, scooped up her products and curling iron and tucked them into her travel bag. "Now, whatever you do, don't put your hat on. Brian wants to shoot some pictures without our hats first."

"Yes, ma'am." He let out another deep sigh. "How long is this shoot gonna take? I've still got chores to do for Miss Petra."

"Not sure. Brian wants some barn shots and others outdoors with the horses." The photographer had already set up his lights in the barn, and June had gotten up early to wash down Sprinter and Shadow, his newish stablemate, so they'd be ready for their close-ups. She was glad her small family ranch had the picturesque scenery Brian liked. She wouldn't remind Raeder that they'd need another photo shoot next week out at the rodeo grounds. Best just to get through today.

"Listen, Raeder, I really appreciate your being such a good sport about all this. I know it's not your thing. But as Everly said yesterday, they're all depending on us to be the face of the rodeo. It means a lot to all of us." The meeting had gone fairly well, with only Alice Austen, the event coordinator, insisting on a few of her favorite picky points.

Raeder shrugged and gave her a crooked grin. "It means a lot to me, too. Gives me a chance to make some serious headway on my return to competing."

"Oh." Her heart dropped. "I thought you'd decided not to…"

"Can't think where you got that idea."

"But aren't you worried that your son—"

"Nope. Never give much space to worry." He reached for his new hat and started to put it on. "Oops. Almost forgot." He set it back in its box. "I guess putting on my hat is second nature."

Had he done that to change the subject?

"Whew. If you messed up your hair with all that hairspray in it, we'd have to wash it and start all over."

"Ugh! Can't go through that again."

They headed out to the barn and met up with Brian Hedley, the rodeo's official photographer, who was explaining to Peanut how the lighting worked. As usual, Brian looked them up and down with a critical eye as he greeted them, his fancy camera hanging on a black strap around his neck.

"Hey, folks. You're looking real good. Let's start over here by the stalls." He waved a hand in the direction of Sprinter's stall.

When the bay gelding saw June, he nickered a greeting and put his head over the side of the stall.

"Hey, big boy." She ran a hand down his nose, and he moved closer. "We'll take you out for a ride in a bit." She glanced at Raeder. "That's Shadow over there…"

Raeder was already approaching the other stall, an undefinable expression on his face. "Hey, fella." He laid his forehead against the dark gray stallion's neck, and the horse nickered as it rubbed against him. "Sure have missed you." His voice held a plaintive note.

"Missed him?" June walked over to them. "How do you know Shadow? Dad bought him last fall… Oh." She'd forgotten the horse had been among the possessions Raeder had had to sell to pay his hospital bill after his injury.

The fond yet rueful expression on his face almost broke her heart.

"It's good to see him so well taken care of."

"Looks like he's glad to see you, too." In the back of her mind, she heard the *click-click* of Brian's camera. Should he be taking pictures of this sweet reunion between Shadow and his former owner? She would speak to him later to be sure he didn't misuse those photos. "Raeder, you can ride him anytime."

A brief look of annoyance crossed his face. Then he shook

it off and seemed to force a smile. "Well, let's get those pictures done. Brian, shoot away."

June had a little trouble pasting on her own rodeo queen smile. Raeder had suffered more than a banged-up knee in last year's rodeo. He'd suffered the loss of a cowboy's best friend, a horse with whom he had a very special relationship. If she ever had to sell Sprinter, whom she'd raised from a newborn colt, she doubted she would ever recover from the loss.

Chapter Three

"I know, boy." Mounted on Sprinter in the alleyway behind the Rodeo de Santa Fe arena, June leaned down and patted her gelding's neck. "Only a few more minutes."

Sprinter didn't like standing still, but he behaved himself today as they waited to make their entrance with the other rodeo queens. June was happy to be here, happy about the great meeting they'd had with the Santa Fe committee yesterday morning before the rodeo's third day. Happy to share the adventure with Raeder, whose humble cowboy demeanor went a long way in impressing these folks to work with Riverton. So different from Bret Hancock's off-putting cockiness, Raeder's personality made him a terrific partner in their shared project.

The only thing she disliked about participating in this four-day event was having to miss teaching her Sunday school class. She only had three more months with her precious preschoolers before they graduated to the kindergarten class. She especially would miss Peanut. He wasn't the first motherless child she'd taught, but in the nine months he'd been her student, he'd claimed a very large portion of her heart. Raeder didn't seem to understand that his son's sucking his thumb at four years old indicated some serious insecurities, but he wasn't exactly open to listening to June's concerns.

Taylor Sandoval, the Rodeo de Santa Fe's middle-aged coordinator, stood in the alleyway leading to the arena and checked down the line of mounted queens. "You ready, ladies?"

"Yes, ma'am," the fourteen riders chorused as a warm June breeze brushed over them, blowing their long, carefully coiffed hair in the wind while not disturbing their safely secured cowgirl hats. Ahead, the sun beamed down on the sandy soil where the competition would soon begin. At this huge rodeo, many state and national queens made appearances to advertise their own hometown events and stir up interest in rodeo among those who hadn't yet discovered all the great excitement of the historical sport.

Taylor gave the signal, the gate opened and the riders began their queen runs one by one as each was announced over the loudspeaker, beginning with several smaller New Mexico rodeos, including June as Miss Riverton Stampede. They rode at breakneck speed around the arena's perimeter, waving to the thousands of cheering fans before finally making a circle at the center. At last, Miss Rodeo de Santa Fe, dressed in crimson, rhinestone-sprinkled Western garb, raced in on her magnificent black Arabian stallion, with the American flag secured in the flag boot attached to her saddle and fluttering majestically in the wind. She took her place in the middle of the other women as the national anthem was sung by a hometown military veteran.

June always loved this moment of every rodeo, whether she was a participant or a spectator. Every time she heard the national anthem, she pictured Old Glory flying over Fort McHenry as the British navy invaded during the War of 1812. How could any red-blooded American fail to appreciate the sacrifice of those brave soldiers and sailors who saved this country in its second war to secure independence? If not for being "on stage," she'd wipe a tear from her eye.

She'd already been deeply moved this morning by the pastor's message at Cowboy Church. Now, as she sat on Sprinter and surveyed the bleachers, where everyone stood and joined in the singing, her heart was flooded with love of God and country.

Glancing across the arena toward the bleachers, she located Raeder, who sat in the front row with some of the rodeo officials, his son on his shoulders, both of them singing their lungs out. Raeder Junior, or RJ, as she'd begun to think of the boy, looked so adorable in his cowboy outfit that matched his dad's, all provided by Boot Barn and Tecovas as part of both businesses' agreements to promote the Riverton Stampede.

The eruption of the staged fireworks interrupted her thoughts, and she rode out of the arena with the other queens to more cheers from the spectators. For her, the excitement had only begun. Halfway through today's events, she and Sprinter would compete in the barrel racing. With an hour to wait, she watched the bareback riders do their best to stay on the bucking broncos for a full eight seconds to qualify for the prize. Their total points would depend on their staying power and the horse's performance. If the animal failed to give enough resistance, the rider earned fewer points for the ride. At the end of the four-day rodeo, the rider with the most points in each event won the big prize money.

She knew she shouldn't watch. Every time a rider was bucked off and barely missed being struck by the horse's hooves, she recalled the day four years ago when Eric had been bucked off a Brahman bull, and his hand got caught in the bucking strap. He'd been dragged for the eternity of ten seconds as the rodeo bullfighters and wranglers on horseback tried to rescue him. Once he managed to free himself, he fell under the bull, which came down on his back. That was the day her opinion of rodeos changed. She still loved some parts of the sport, but not the life-threatening dangerous ones. Why would a healthy young man engage in such a dangerous sport when he didn't need to? Or if he had responsibilities to a wife or children? Why not take up a relatively safer event, like calf roping or even steer wrestling?

Without meaning to, she located Raeder in the stands again. Even at a distance, she could see him watching the riders with intense interest. Was it because he'd done so well as a bull-riding champion for eight years and appreciated what today's riders were experiencing? She hated that he wanted to ride again. What would happen to little RJ if the worst happened to his father? Had he made a will and designated a guardian for his son? How had he planned to provide for his son in the event that he no longer could?

Barrel racing came right before intermission, and June would be the fourth rider. She always made it a rule never to watch her competition, but she couldn't avoid hearing her competitors' riding times. The girl who rode before her came in with a thirteen-point-two time, and June's competitive nature kicked into overdrive.

"Come on, Sprinter. Let's do this."

She dug in her spurs, and they raced out of the chute and rounded each of the three barrels without so much as brushing them, finally galloping at breakneck speed from the farthest barrel to the finish line.

As with every rider, noisy cheers, whistles and applause of support thundered in the bleachers. June knew she had a few fans out there in addition to Mom and Dad…and maybe RJ. She was just glad she and Sprinter hadn't knocked over a single barrel.

"Thirteen-point-three seconds!" the announcer called out.

For the briefest moment, she was disappointed. Then she laughed at herself. If she came in second or third, or didn't even place, it was okay. Let the ones with a desperate need for winning take the top prize. She only rode to please her family and to keep up the Mattson tradition. Besides, hadn't she recently decided not to compete in rodeos after the busyness of her queen year ended? Even before that, she needed to buckle down and complete her undergraduate pre-vet degree. Then she would move on to earning her doctorate in veterinary medicine. Dad and Mom had a friendly competition of their own, each trying to persuade her to join their veterinary practice. When the day came, June trusted that the Lord would show her which one to choose. In the meantime, she would just keep her dear parents guessing.

Peanut hollered and bounced around so much Raeder had to set him down off his shoulders as they watched June race around the barrels. "That's my Sunday school teacher! Miss June! Miss June!"

His high-pitched voice was nearly drowned out amid the thunderous noise of the crowd cheering on her ride, but that didn't stop his excitement. When she crossed the finish post, he yelled, "Did Miss June win, Daddy? Did she win?"

The announcer gave her time, only a tenth of a second over the previous rider.

"She did real good, buddy." Raeder admired her horsemanship and the way she cut real close around those barrels without touching them. He hoped she wasn't too disappointed not to have the fastest ride. Sometimes it took only a fraction of a second to win an event. Today, none of the following riders had better times, yet every single one received the same cheers and applause. Or sympathetic groans when a barrel went down.

Raeder knew from experience that rodeo fans were the most generous supporters in the world. While competition was the name of the game, nobody booed or held a grudge, as sometimes happened in some other sports. But like those other sports, once a competitor was knocked out of the game, they could easily be forgotten as new challengers came along. Raeder still had a few fans who remembered him. He remained friends with men he'd ridden against, but they all had to move on with their own lives, not stick around and coddle him. Yet when he spoke to several friends before today's rodeo, they welcomed him back and encouraged his plans to compete again.

Watching the bull riding had been excruciating. He knew them all. Prayed for them as they rode. Knew what they were experiencing. He could feel his grip on the woven bucking strap, could feel the marking out of his legs above the bull's shoulders, could feel the whoosh of the chute gate opening, could feel every buck, every jarring of his head, as the rider was thrown around like a ragdoll, and every thud of the hooves on the ground. Every painful fall to the arena's dirt floor. Every barely missed kick of a hoof as the bull tore away from its rider as the bullfighters diverted its attention. And despite that time last year, when ol' Spite and Malice came down on his left knee and nearly crippled him for life, Raeder missed it more than words could express.

Lord, You have to let me ride this event again. You have to let me conquer the fear that's trying to grab hold of me. If I don't beat it, it'll beat me. If I don't beat it, it'll turn me into a quitter. For Peanut's sake, help me to be a man he can be proud of.

At intermission, he and Peanut ate their overpriced hot

dogs and sodas. Then, thumb in mouth, the little rascal fell asleep halfway through the rodeo's classic event, saddle bronc riding. By the time they got home, it would be late, and they'd miss supper at Miss Petra's. Raeder had already finished his share of business with the Santa Fe committee, and June would be going back to Riverton with her horse and her family. So, eager to avoid the rush at the end of the night's events, Raeder carried Peanut up the stairs to the exit, thankful his injured leg had improved so he no longer needed his cane to manage the concrete steps.

After the surgeon mended his torn ACL, MCL and meniscus tendons, he'd had to work hard in physical therapy to gradually bend his knee so the scar tissue didn't grow together and prevent the knee from ever bending again. When his insurance ran out, he'd had to keep up the torture of exercise on his own. But the Lord had enabled him. At least he'd been able to purchase the eight-hundred-dollar brace that protected him from accidentally bending his knee too far, too fast. He'd finally dispensed with the brace, and now, he was pretty close to being able to bend it to a healthy 130 degrees. Next would come practicing his rides on the mechanical bull at Raintree Restaurant in Riverton, in the off hours, of course.

Being hired by Miss Petra had been a gift from the Lord. Working around the ranch, he had to push himself to do the necessary tasks to keep the place going. At first, milking had been the hardest because he couldn't bend his injured knee to sit on the low stool. To his relief, both milk cows, Chloe and Maude, were agreeable to letting him slide his injured leg underneath them while he relieved them of the weight of their twice-daily production of milk. Hauling in hay bales to feed the gals, a task he'd done with ease on his parents' small ranch in Wyoming, also offered a challenge.

So he broke up the bales and used the wheelbarrow to bring the hay into the stalls.

At first, the trials of healing and getting the ranch work done, plus taking care of Peanut, demanded all his attention and physical effort. After attending today's rodeo, he felt greatly encouraged to get back in the saddle and further strengthen his damaged leg so he could indeed enter the Riverton Stampede in October. Just the thought of it made his pulse kick up.

Across the fence of the parking lot outside the arena, he saw the rodeo queens lining up again for their final ride to close out the evening's event. His eyes went right to a certain blonde on a certain high-priced, registered bay horse. As always, June looked real good. Looked like a real cowgirl. Which she was. She'd shone like a star when they'd met with the Santa Fe committee yesterday, and he'd let her do most of the talking.

June looked his way and waved. Even though they'd been together yesterday morning at the meeting and this morning at Cowboy Church, he glanced behind himself to be sure he was her target, because nothing was as embarrassing as waving back at somebody who was waving at somebody else. His quick glance showed only a few folks heading to their cars, so he risked the wave with his free hand. By that time, she'd already turned away and was riding into the arena with the other gals.

He chuckled at his own foolishness. As he constantly had to remind himself, despite their promotional work together for the Riverton Stampede, June Mattson was far above him socially and economically. Plus, she was a little bossy when it came to thinking she knew what his son needed. As if Raeder didn't have Peanut's best interests front and center in all his thoughts.

He'd already taught his son to read and write. Peanut knew his colors and basic addition, important skills when it came to raising his chickens. The pullets they'd purchased in the early spring as baby chicks had started laying, and Peanut could already tell which hen laid which eggs. He could spout all sorts of details about caring for his chickens. He and Sassy shared the responsibility of feeding and watering the critters, and he insisted on helping her clean out the coop and add new straw, much to her annoyance when that straw got spread far and wide over the chicken yard. Raeder had to stifle his laughter when Sassy huffed and fussed over having to pick up after his son.

Raeder was determined to teach Peanut every skill required to work on a ranch, beginning with the responsibility of those chickens. But as Peanut got older, could Raeder teach him everything else he needed for a well-rounded, well-educated life? Maybe June's idea about enrolling Peanut in kindergarten in town wasn't so bad after all.

On second thought, that didn't sit well with Raeder. Not even a little bit. How could he ensure Peanut had a good teacher, one who understood he didn't have a mama and needed a gentle hand? No, June had it all wrong. Raeder would go online tonight and order the books he needed to bring his son up to scratch to equal any kid in Riverton Elementary School.

If Miss June Mattson didn't approve, she'd just have to deal with it.

Seated two rows back on the right side of the sanctuary with other members of the Mattson clan, June watched little RJ enter through the double doors and walk down the center aisle carrying a white pillow with two silk-ribbon-tied wedding rings attached. Head held high, RJ looked entirely adorable in his tan jeans, white dress shirt, blue vest and bolo tie as he walked purposefully toward the front to the music of Pachelbel's "Canon in D Major." Halfway down to the altar, he stopped and turned around. "Come on, Sassy!"

Muted chuckles swept through the room as Sassy, in her frilly pink dress, came through the door tossing white rose petals from her basket a little higher than necessary. "You're supposed to keep walking, Peanut!"

As if he only now realized he was the center of everyone's attention, his eyes widened. "You come with me."

Sassy huffed impatiently. "Okay. Let's go."

Side by side, the two children made their way toward the front, with Peanut using one hand to clutch the pillow and the other to help Sassy toss the flowers.

With so many relatives to choose from—and possibly to offend those who were left out—Sam and Juliet had opted for a small wedding party, with each having only one attendant, plus the children. Of course, Sam chose his law partner, Cousin Will, as his best man, while Juliet had asked Jenna Williams, a cousin from Colorado, to be her maid of honor. While the bride's side of the sanctuary didn't have as many relatives in attendance as Sam's, she had a respectable number of friends who filled the pews.

When the children neared the front, RJ saw June. "Hi, Miss June." He took the remaining few rose petals from Sassy's basket and handed them to her. "Here. These are for you."

More chuckles filled the sanctuary as June's face warmed. "Thank you," she whispered.

Across the aisle in the front pew, Miss Petra, Juliet's mother, gave June a teasing grin.

The wedding ceremony couldn't have had a better beginning, except for a slight delay of the bride's entrance. June noticed Cousin Sam's nervous shifting, unusual for his normally cool disposition. Finally, the organist played the first bars of Mendelssohn's "Wedding March," and Miss Petra stood, followed by the rest of the room, to watch Juliet enter.

No bride could have been prettier. She wore a Western-style lace dress, white rhinestone-covered boots any rodeo queen would envy and a brimmed Stetson hat covered with a veil that draped down her sides and back. She walked slowly down the aisle on the arm of her teenage brother, Jeff. Jeff and Juliet had the same father, Dill Sizemore, but different mothers, and Dill was in prison for murdering Jeff's mother, Brenda. After that difficult history, the siblings deserved some happiness.

June had never spent much time dreaming of and planning her own eventual wedding, as some of her friends had done. But today, she thought it must be wonderful for a woman to walk down the aisle toward the man she loved, the man she wanted to spend the rest of her life with. Not meaning to, she glanced across the aisle again to where Raeder sat on Petra's other side. He was also looking at her, but quickly looked away when their eyes met. No, not Raeder. She could never pledge her life to a man with a child who insisted on going back to the sport that had almost killed him.

Under a cottonwood tree on the church's back lawn, Raeder sat with Peanut on plastic chairs amid several hundred people enjoying a barbecue reception in honor of Sam and Juliet's wedding. He brushed white cake crumbs and a smidgeon of white frosting from Peanut's new blue vest Miss Petra had made. She'd done a lot of sewing for her daughter's wedding, so Raeder appreciated her adding his son's outfit to her list. These clothes would look sharp for Peanut to wear to Sunday school in place of the well-worn jeans and shirt

Raeder had found at the thrift shop. With his son growing so fast, he needed the next size up all too often.

Across the yard, June chatted with Juliet, a bride so pretty, she looked like she'd stepped out of a fashion magazine. Raeder laughed at himself over having such an idea. Before those miserable rodeo photo shoots with Brian, who today was going around taking the wedding pictures, he'd never thought much about how magazine models appeared, or even how pictures of himself turned out. The only photo he had of his own wedding was a snapshot Audra's sister had taken with her phone. Still, it was good enough for a printout, which he treasured and often showed Peanut so he'd remember his mama.

Unlike today's fancy do, Raeder and Audra's wedding had been a private affair at the preacher's house, with only Ma, Audra's single mom and younger sister, and the preacher and his wife in attendance. Pa, being his usual self, didn't bother to show up. They'd had no decorations, like the fancy fripperies festooning the churchyard today, just a bunch of flowers from a neighbor's yard for Audra's bridal bouquet and a dandelion he'd stuck in his shirt lapel for a boutonniere at the last minute. Their wedding refreshments had been cupcakes from the local grocery-store bakery. Yet they'd been every bit as married as Juliet and Sam were today. Every bit as blissfully happy as two immature, inexperienced eighteen-year-olds could be. They'd both grown up a whole heap after having Peanut and then through Audra's cancer journey. Raeder swallowed down unexpected emotion as he ruminated on those days. In the past four years, the sharp pain of his grief had faded into a persistent dull ache as he'd been forced to get on with life, somehow managing to care for Peanut while establishing himself as a bull rider with increasing success. He'd often thought he'd gladly trade that success to have Audra back, but now, he didn't even have that. All the more reason to get back in the arena and conquer his fears and doubts, not to mention rebuild his self-esteem. And set a good example for his son.

"Hey, Peanut." Sassy danced over to them in her usual perky fashion, trailed by Will's two little kids, Jemmy and Emily. "Want to play kickball with us?" She looked at Raeder. "Can he come play kickball with us in the gym? I'll take care of him."

Raeder appreciated her asking permission. At ten years old, she'd come a long way since last Christmas, when she and Juliet had moved to Miss Petra's ranch. "You want to go?" he asked his son.

Peanut answered by jumping down from his chair and grasping Sassy's offered hand. And away they skipped, along with a huge piece of Raeder's heart. His son meant everything to him. How would the little guy manage once Sassy moved to the Double Bar M Ranch on the far side of Riverton? Raeder would need to keep him close and homeschool him to help him feel secure.

Sam wandered over and sat in the chair Peanut had vacated. "Whew! Glad that's over."

Raeder chuckled. "I'm sure you are. Waiting at the altar, you looked about as nervous as a long-tailed cat in a roomful of rocking chairs."

Sam snorted out a laugh. "Yep. That about sums it up." He gazed across the room toward his bride, and his expression grew tender. "It took us ten years to get here, but here we are, thank the Good Lord."

"Amen to that. Where're you going for your honeymoon?" He and Audra had managed one night at a mountain resort, courtesy of Ma. No doubt this newest Mattson couple could afford better.

"Shh." Sam held a finger up to his lips. "State secret." He shifted in his chair. "Can you do me a favor and keep an eye on Sassy while we're gone? Miss Petra's going to babysit her, but Jeff'll be working at the hardware store over the summer. It would be great to have another set of eyes on her."

"No problem. That'll postpone Peanut's disappointment when she moves away."

"Aw, man. I hope he's going to be okay."

"He'll be fine. He's used to big changes." At least Raeder prayed he'd be okay.

"Listen, I came over here to congratulate you on the fine job you and Cousin June are doing for the rodeo. I've talked to Will, and we want you to put our law office on your list of sponsors."

Raeder sat back, grinning. "Wow. That's awesome." More than awesome. With the Mattson law firm and the Mattson's Double Bar M Ranch as two sponsors, maybe even more local business would be encouraged to add their support.

Almost like she'd heard her name mentioned, June hurried over and gave Sam a big hug. "Cousin Will just told me you're going to sponsor the rodeo."

Sam laughed as he returned the hug. "How could we not sponsor it after all of us pestered you to compete for the Miss Riverton Stampede title? Gotta support our little cousin. Gotta make our little town proud by keeping a ninety-three-year-old event going." He stood. "Looks like my bride's trying to get my attention. I think she's gonna throw her bouquet. I'd better get over there. You coming, Junebug?"

"Nope." She plopped down in the chair.

"You don't want to try to catch it?" Sam gave her a teasing smirk.

"Nope," she repeated.

"Suit yourself." He chuckled as he trotted away.

Raeder laughed, too. "I thought every unmarried gal was supposed to join in the fun."

"Humph. Not me. I have too much going for me to think about marriage. Finish my queen year and college classes. Graduate. Go to vet school."

"Huh. Sounds like a pretty serious plan."

"It is." She slid him a sidelong glance. "What about you? Any plans for after our rodeo?"

Sensing true interest, he decided to risk sharing some ideas.

"Sure. I've got plenty." He already knew she didn't think much of his plan to compete in bull riding, so he'd leave that part out. "I've got some riding students lined up for when your dad gives the okay to put Darby to work. He's doing much better with the Adequan injections. 'Course, I'll keep on running the ranch for Miss Petra. And she's given me the okay to set up a machine shop for repairing farm machinery. As I told you a while back, I have a trade-school degree in machine repair." He didn't know why he added that last bit. Pride, maybe? To remind her he wasn't a high-school dropout or something. "And I'll be homeschooling Peanut. Already sent for the kindergarten books."

She did fine listening to him with a smile until that last bit. Now she frowned and shook her head. "Hmm. Well, I'm real glad to hear about Darby. How about I come out and have a look at him on Monday? Maybe he's ready for those riding lessons."

"Sounds good."

Laughter and squeals sounded from across the lawn, where one of the young ladies had caught Miss Juliet's bouquet. Raeder pondered the idea of June not participating in the entertaining wedding ritual. Maybe she already had a beau. Maybe one of those cowboys she chatted with at the

Rodeo de Santa Fe. If he was somebody local, surely Miss Petra would have said something, kindhearted but a bit gossipy as she was. And somehow, the idea of June Mattson having a boyfriend just didn't sit right with Raeder, though he couldn't imagine why.

Chapter Four

For the third time, Raeder picked himself up from the padded flooring beneath the mechanical bull and shook off the muted pain traveling through his body. He'd expected it to be easier to get back into shape. In addition to exercising his left leg, he'd been working on his core—a key part of staying on a live bull—and every other muscle in his body. But after today, he could see the whole experience would require more serious work for him to regain his balance and ability to hang on for an eight-second ride.

Could he reclaim the skill he'd built up over his career by October? Instinctively remember techniques that had become second nature to him through the years? Recall the expertise it took to read the bull and anticipate its twists and turns? Whatever had happened to the idea of never forgetting how to ride a bicycle? Shouldn't that apply to bull riding?

"Ready to speed it up?" Cody Martinez, the fortysomething restaurant owner, rested his arms on top of the padded railing surrounding the bull-riding pen.

Raeder chuckled. "Not quite. Gimme a few more tries."

"Take your time." Cody waved a hand toward the wall where a clock framed with horns from a Texas Longhorn hung. "We open in about an hour, and I won't let anybody in until then. And just so you know—" he winked "—I made my staff promise to keep your practice a secret."

"I appreciate it, pal." Raeder more than appreciated it. As a former bull rider himself, Cody hadn't asked for payment or publicity for his generosity. He'd even signed up as one of the rodeo sponsors, saying he wanted to do his share to keep the stampede going for another ninety-three years. Raeder looked forward to telling June about this new sponsor just to see the light in those bright blue eyes.

Though Cody hadn't said it, Raeder suspected the man wanted him to succeed in his comeback, where he himself had failed fifteen or so years ago. That went a long way to demonstrate what a good man and a good friend he was. When Raeder had just been starting out, he had heard of Cody's successes. Pictures on the restaurant walls recalled his glory days, when he'd almost reached the top of their shared sport. Other pictures, all autographed, showcased other riders at their best. Raeder had never gone much for the publicity photos like some of his fellow bull riders did, but he'd sure try to dig one up to give Cody to show his appreciation. Raeder probably had a few copies of one action shot taken by Bill Jacobs, official photographer of the Ski Hi Stampede in Monte Vista, Colorado, three years ago. His posture had been perfect, with his legs in position, right arm in the air and hat still on his head, while the bull had both front hooves on the ground and back hooves kicking high. Some folks called the photo iconic for the sport. It even ended up in a national rodeo magazine. Bill had sent Raeder a stack of eight-by-ten glossies, and for the last two years at the same rodeo, he'd signed them with a Sharpie and handed them out to fans and a few friends.

After another half hour of practice on the fake bull, Raeder managed to stay on for the full eight seconds, plus a few extra seconds for good measure. He glanced at the clock. Better get back to Miss Petra's ranch so he could get busy cutting the alfalfa after lunch.

As he headed to his Bronco, he counted fewer bruises than he'd expected on his bare arms. At least he'd hadn't forgotten how to do a rolling fall when tossed off the machine. And at least he hadn't given up. So much for his father's frequent dismissals of everything Raeder had ever tried, calling him a quitter and a loser. Ma had tried to make up for it by her constant cheerleading when Pa wasn't within hearing distance. But a boy needed his father's approval and encouragement, so Peanut would never hear a discouraging word from him. For the first time, Raeder had the fleeting thought that maybe June was right about calling his son *Peanut*. No, it was what Audra had called the little guy, so that was good enough for both father and son. Besides, making the change would confuse Peanut, something Raeder tried never to do.

As he drove toward the ranch, he called Miss Petra. "Ma'am, you need anything at the store?"

"Don't think so, son." She paused. "Well, you might bring a treat for Peanut. He's a little mopey this morning. Sassy's folks are back from their honeymoon. They've already packed her up and moved her over to the Double Bar M." She gave out a sad little laugh. "I'm a little mopey about it myself. It was so good to have my daughter and granddaughter living here with me. Don't know what I'll do if you and Peanut move away."

Raeder felt his own heart ping, and not in a good way. "Miss Petra, I don't know what we'd do without you. You've made a home for us." He swallowed hard before his emotions got the better of him. "We ain't...aren't going anywhere."

"I'm glad to hear it. Now, on a happier note, June called to say she's coming out to check on Darby."

Raeder couldn't miss the teasing in her tone. "Hmm.

Yeah, well, I'll stop at the store and get something for Peanut to get his mind off of Sassy's move."

Miss Petra laughed out loud. "You do that, son. I'll tell him…and June, too, that you're on your way."

"Thanks." Raeder disconnected the call without further comment. Miss Petra's matchmaking attempts bounced off him like…well, actually, they dug in like a spur. Couldn't the dear woman see he and June weren't a good match? Not that June's parents, Eli and Sue, showed him any disrespect, but he knew enough not to set his sights that high. Pa's disapproval and constant berating might not have kept Raeder from succeeding at bull riding, but it had solidified his belief that he should never marry outside of his place in this world. He was a blue-collar, trade-school man, while June was working toward becoming a doctor of veterinary medicine. And Raeder wouldn't court any woman just to be courting. If he did decide to spend time with someone of the fairer gender, she had to be someone who would make a good mama for Peanut.

Such thoughts always circled back around to June and the way she and Peanut had taken to each other. They had these next few months until Peanut graduated to kindergarten Sunday school class and the two months after that when they continued to promote the rodeo. Then Raeder could avoid her for the rest of his life.

All these thoughts were foolish. June was bound to find some cowboy, or maybe a big-time rancher or a lawyer like her cousins. Or maybe another veterinarian, a man more qualified to marry a lady of her prominence. That idea should settle the matter for him, but it only made him sad.

June listened to Darby's chest and belly just like Dad had taught her from the time she was eight years old. Everything sounded good. A steady heartbeat and healthy rumbling in the gelding's stomach. She patted his rump, then started to put away her stethoscope. Glancing toward the hay bale outside Darby's stall, she noticed little RJ's bright-eyed interest.

"Want to take a listen?" She held out the stethoscope.

"Uh-huh." Without hesitation, he jumped down from the bale and hopped over to the stall.

"Careful, honey." She gently grasped his shoulder. "Darby likes you, but he's also big and heavy, and sometimes shifts around without warning. Stand here and listen." She put one earpiece up to his ear and the resonator against Darby's side. "What do you hear?"

His brown eyes serious, he said, "Tump-tump, tump-tump."

"That's his heart. Does it sound okay to you?"

He scrunched up his forehead. "I think so." He eyed her with a sober expression. "We don't listen to our chickens' hearts."

"I see." She chuckled. "Okay, now, tell me what you hear." She placed the resonator against Darby's large belly, moving it around to random spots.

RJ giggled. "Rumble, rumble. Like my daddy's belly when he's hungry."

Not wanting to hop on that silly train of thought, June managed to contain her own laugh. "I think we all have rumbling bellies when we're hungry. What's important about Darby is that those sounds mean he's healthy." She put the stethoscope into her black bag. "Now, let's take a look at his legs." She lifted each hoof, testing the bend of the legs, allowing RJ to run his small hand across each joint. Darby complied in his usual placid manner, giving no indication of any resistance or pain. "Good job, big boy." To RJ, she said, "That medicine your daddy's giving him is working."

"Add-a-can." He spoke with serious conviction.

Nodding, she pursed her lips to again smother a laugh. His mispronunciations were so cute! "Very good. Yes, the Adequan is working." Which was exactly what Raeder had told her the other day. Not that she doubted him. He knew how to read horses, but her dad wanted her to check.

When she'd arrived at Miss Petra's ranch a half hour ago, she'd been disappointed not to see Raeder's Bronco parked outside the house, because she wanted to discuss the upcoming weekend promotional trip after checking on Darby. Before she'd climbed out of her pickup, RJ had run out of the house and thrown himself into her arms.

"Miss June, Sassy's gone far away forever," he'd wailed.

"Oh, no, honey. She's just moved a few miles away." She'd brushed tears from his cheek. "You can play with her lots of times." Noticing Miss Petra standing on the back stoop, she'd waved. The dear lady had looked a little sad herself. "I'll watch RJ… I mean, Peanut, if you like." She needed to watch what she called the little guy.

"Thanks, honey. I do need to get a few things done." Miss Petra had then ducked back inside the house.

Meanwhile, RJ had sniffed back his tears. "Now I have to take care of the chickens all by myself."

"Well, let's go take a look to see what they need."

And so they'd spent a few minutes checking the water and gathering eggs. The tender care this little boy had taken with the eggs surprised her, and yet it hadn't, she thought now. His dad was careful with the ranch animals, which went along with his laid-back personality. Well, except in the matter of bull riding. The contradiction never ceased to puzzle her. Why did he feel compelled to return to the arena? And why did she keep worrying that he would actually do it?

As if her thoughts had summoned him, Raeder's Bronco

drove slowly down the lane from the highway, and her heart hiccupped. Why on earth? She saw the man all the time. Today was no different.

He parked by the house and climbed out of the vehicle, so June took RJ by the hand.

"There's your daddy."

With a happy squeal, the boy pulled away and dashed across the barnyard. "Daddy!"

June followed him, ready to report her diagnosis of Darby. Raeder had said he was eager to start riding lessons, so she had good news for him.

Raeder set down the plastic Mattsons' Garden and Hardware bag he was carrying and reached out to gather his son in his arms, then swung him around to the sounds of more squeals, at last setting him back on his feet and squatting beside him. He grabbed the bag and held it out.

"Want to see what I got you?"

"Yeah!" RJ snatched it and peered inside, then pulled out a plastic toy tool set hanging from a braided bright blue-and-yellow nylon belt and grinned. "So cool." He threw his arms around Raeder's neck, almost knocking him over. "Thank you, thank you."

Raeder chuckled, his baritone voice tender with affection.

Watching father and son interact always brought joy to June's heart. Raeder was doing a remarkable job as a single parent.

"Here," he said to RJ. "Let me help you put it on." He adjusted the belt length, then hung it around RJ's waist. "There you go. Pretty sharp. Now, you got everything you need to help me around the ranch. Hammer, ruler, saw, wrench." He glanced up and when he saw June his eyes flickered with… interest? Surprise? "Hey there. How's Darby?" He stood and shuffled his feet awkwardly. "Sorry. Should have asked how you're doing first."

Like most cowboys, he was pretty cute when he was embarrassed. Though, if she was being honest with herself, she'd say he was cuter than most cowboys she knew, with those intense brown eyes and tousled, curly blond hair. She stepped closer, noticing he also looked a little scruffy. What had he been up to? "I'm fine. Darby's fine, too. In fact, I think we should take him out for a ride to see how he takes to the trail. I can trailer Shadow over here and load him up for a ride down by the river." She waved a hand in the direction of the Rio Grande, some two miles away.

At the mention of Shadow, he winced slightly but seemed to force a smile. "Sounds like a plan."

Another little hiccup bounced near her heart. She hadn't thought about how it might cause him pain to ride the horse he used to own. Too late to reconsider the idea, so she forged ahead. "Great. Maybe next week after we get back from Albuquerque?" They would be speaking to the NMBRA— New Mexico Barrel Racing Association—about adding the Riverton Stampede to their roster to attract some of the top barrel racers.

"Sounds like a plan," he repeated. "Can you bring Shadow's saddle? I don't have one for him here."

"Sure. Do you have one for Darby?"

"Yeah. There was an old one in the barn from way back in the olden days. I cleaned it up so I can use it for lessons."

She gave him a questioning grin. "The olden days?"

"Yeah. Way back when Miss Petra's great-great-grandparents settled on this land."

"Wow, that is way back. You sure the saddle's okay?"

"Yep. Wouldn't use it for kids if it wasn't."

"No. Of course not." Her cheeks heated up. She knew better than to question a cowboy's care for his tack.

"Daddy, Miss June let me listen to Darby's tummy."

"She did?" He raised one eyebrow. "Maybe I should have got you a kid's doctor kit instead?" He gave RJ's new favorite toy a critical look.

"Oh, no," June said. "Every child needs to learn how to use hammers and saws. I'm sure RJ—" *Oops.* "I'm sure Peanut will have fun with those."

Raeder narrowed his eyes. "RJ?"

Again, heat flooded her cheeks. "Well… I, uh…" She sighed. Might as well confess. "Yes, RJ. Raeder Junior. That's the way I think of him now. He's so much more than a…" She glanced at the little guy, who was already engrossed in his new tool belt, then leaned close to Raeder and whispered, "So much more than a peanut. Why not call him by his initials? Lots of guys, even girls, go by initials these days."

He stepped back and stared at her for several seconds, conflict warring in his expression. "Don't let me keep you. I'm sure you have more horses and other critters to check on." He squatted back down by his son. "Let's go inside and show your new toy to Miss Petra. I'm guessing she has our lunch about ready." He glanced at June and touched the brim of his hat. "Ma'am," he said before taking RJ's hand and heading toward the house.

Well, that didn't go like I'd hoped. She blew out a long sigh and turned back toward the barn to get her equipment. As she loaded up her pickup, she saw another vehicle navigating the ranch's bumpy entrance lane, pulling a horse trailer. Zeke Baldwin must be coming to court Miss Petra. Too bad the dear lady didn't return his interest.

After climbing into her own ride, she drove toward the lane and pulled to the right to give Zeke room to pass. The sixtysomething gentleman waved her to a stop, so she rolled down her window.

"Yessir?"

"Hey, June. You got a minute? Maybe two or three? I got this old donkey in the trailer that I brought to keep company with Darby. Found out they were stablemates a few years back. Thought I'd see if Miss Petra would mind boarding him for me. I know your pappy taught you just about everything he knows, so do you mind checking him over?"

"Sure. I'd love to." If June needed a pick-me-up after Raeder dismissed her, however gently, this was it. She could give the donkey an initial checkup and have Dad look him over more in-depth next time he came out to see Darby.

She waited until Zeke drove on toward the barn, then did a U-turn to follow him. Raeder and Miss Petra must have heard the noise of the vehicles, because they came out of the house and joined them, with RJ tagging along behind.

"What'cha got there, Zeke?" Miss Petra's floral apron and jeans bore a dusting of wheat flour, probably from her latest round of baking. June's stomach growled at the aroma of fresh bread swirling around the woman.

"W-e-e-l-l…let me show you." He walked to the back of the trailer, unlatched the trailer's gate and climbed in, emerging with a placid-looking reddish-gray donkey. "This here's Rusty. He's Darby's old pal from back in the day. Hey, Raeder," he called out as Raeder stepped closer to join them. "Say, you and June here sure have been doing great work for the stampede. We appreciate it."

"You're welcome." Raeder seemed reluctant to look at June. Was he still annoyed with her for calling his son RJ?

"Yep." Zeke turned his attention to Miss Petra. "Now, Miss Petra, ma'am, I don't want you to worry about nothin'. I'm just wantin' to board Rusty here for a bit while I do some renovations to my barn. I'll pay his expenses. That okay with you?"

Miss Petra snorted out a laugh. "Looks like you've gone and decided the matter." She shook her head and looked at Raeder. "What do you think?"

Cowboy cute as ever, he scratched behind his ear. "I kinda like the idea. Donkeys are real good at keeping away predators, so maybe Rusty can protect Peanut's chicken coop."

Zeke's light brown eyes lit up. "Yeah, yeah. That, too. Now, June here has agreed to take a look-see at him to make sure he's healthy. Don't want to put a sickly critter with Darby. You got time, June?"

He'd already asked her that, but she didn't let on. "Sure. Let me get my gear from my truck."

To her surprise, Raeder followed her and opened the truck door for her. "Listen, June, I'm sorry I was rude to you a while ago." His sorrowful expression backed up his words. "My mama didn't raise me that way. Can you forgive me?"

Oh, my. She took a deep breath and turned away so he wouldn't see the wide grin spreading across her face. "Sure. Of course. No problem." She grabbed her bag and closed the truck door. "Okay, let's go take a look at that little donkey."

Chapter Five

After June gave a listen to Rusty's heart and belly, and generally checked him all over, she declared him in good health. Raeder led the donkey into the barn, with everyone following behind. As they neared Darby's stall, the gelding nickered in recognition, so Raeder paused and let the two animals greet each other nose-to-nose, then rub the sides of their heads together.

"That's so sweet." June came closer and ran a hand over Rusty's back. "They haven't forgotten each other. Look at how Darby's perking up."

"Rusty, too," Raeder said. "Looks like they'll be their own little herd. Now I'll feel better about letting Darby out to graze in the pasture with his pal at his side." With coyotes and pumas frequenting the area, he'd been concerned about leaving the gelding to himself.

Zeke brought a bundle of hay to the stall beside Darby's and filled the water bucket from the hose. "That should take care of him for now."

As soon as they guided the donkey into his own stall, both animals stuck their heads over the front sides to continue their reunion.

"Now, Miss Petra, I think I smelled something mighty good coming from your house," Zeke said, "so y'all were pro'bly 'bout to eat. When you're done, you and I can talk about financial arrangements."

"Oh, honestly, Zeke, you're so transparent." Miss Petra scowled at him, but Raeder thought he saw a glint of humor in her eyes. "You come on in and have some lunch with us." She glanced at June. "You, too, honey. Unless you have other plans."

June blinked those blue eyes in surprise. She glanced at Raeder. Did she think she needed his approval? Of course she didn't. "No, no plans."

"Please stay, Miss June." Peanut released himself from Miss Petra's firm hold and grabbed June's hand. "Please?"

She gave him that sweet smile of hers. "Sure. I'd love to."

After checking to be sure the animals were settling in, they all trooped over to the ranch house, where June jumped right in to help Miss Petra get the meal on the table.

Raeder took Peanut to the mudroom sink to wash his hands. He'd made a small stool for his son to climb up on to reach the faucet, so he stepped back to let the boy do it himself. He did a pretty good job with only a few splashes of water ending up on his T-shirt.

Once they'd all found their places around the kitchen table and Zeke thanked the Lord for His bounty, Raeder helped Peanut serve himself a handful of potato chips from the basket Miss Petra had passed to him. She'd made chicken salad, one of Raeder's favorites, but not Peanut's. Raeder bribed his son to eat the meat mixed with pickles, eggs and mayonnaise by saying he could have one potato chip for each bite he ate. Raeder made a sandwich with his servings of the chicken.

Across the table, June watched their interaction with interest. Was she as concerned about what Peanut ate as she was about his name? Raeder would have to keep an eye out—or maybe an ear out, if that was even a thing—to make sure she didn't confuse Peanut with that new nickname she'd come up with.

Count on Miss Petra to invite June to stay for lunch. 'Course, she was probably just adding another lady to the party for her own benefit after Zeke had practically invited himself. Zeke had made his affection for Miss Petra known for as long as Raeder had been around here, but the woman was having none of it. Sort of made Raeder chuckle, privately, of course, that the lady who was set on acting like a matchmaker for him and June refused the same favor for herself. But he couldn't bring himself to laugh at Zeke's sincerity. He was a good, caring man and really smart when it came to his share of organizing the rodeo.

"Miss Petra," Zeke said around a mouthful, "this is mighty good chicken salad. Only thing missing is a bit of jalapeño to spice it up."

She rolled her eyes and shook her head. "Shows how much you know. Can't serve spicy food like that to little kids. Right, Raeder?" She tilted her head toward Peanut.

"Yes, ma'am." Raeder nodded his appreciation, then shot a grin at Zeke. "Though I wouldn't turn down jalapeño in just about anything for myself."

As the meal went on, June chatted about this and that with Miss Petra, maybe understanding her unusually quiet mood was caused by the departure of Juliet, Sassy and Juliet's brother, Jeff. To Raeder's way of thinking, Miss Petra had been real good to take Jeff in after his father was sent to prison for murdering Jeff's mother. Miss Petra always said it wasn't the boy's fault his daddy left her for another woman.

"Y'know," June said, "maybe Raeder and R—Peanut should move into the house with you."

While Miss Petra's face lit up, Raeder's shock and surprise surely must have registered on his face, along with a pinch of annoyance. Not only was she meddling, but she'd also almost called Peanut RJ.

"Oh, now, we don't want to intrude."

"Nonsense." Miss Petra's grin was wide. "That's a mighty fine idea, June. Raeder, it would be so good to have you closer than way out in the bunkhouse. And now that Sassy's moved away, it'd be easier for me to keep an eye on Peanut when you're out in the field."

"And I'd feel better," said Zeke, "knowing Miss Petra wasn't all alone in the house at night."

Miss Petra rolled her eyes and shook her head—again— then turned to Raeder. "What do you say?"

As the idea settled in his thoughts, he started to like it. The bunkhouse was old and rustic and hard to heat in the winter and cool in summer, not to mention it had spotty lighting for when he read to Peanut in the evenings. 'Course, they always had fun huddling under a blanket tent and using a flashlight to see their storybooks, but Raeder wasn't sure that was good for Peanut's eyes.

"Sounds like a fine idea, ma'am. Thank you."

Miss Petra chuckled. "You should thank June for coming up with the idea." She tilted her head toward June and winked at him.

At the other end of the table, Zeke laughed out loud. He'd already made himself a nuisance with veiled suggestions about Raeder and June, so Raeder had learned to ignore his hints.

"Yes, ma'am. Thanks, June." If Raeder had been wearing a dress shirt and tie instead of a T-shirt, he'd be tugging at his collar. Time to divert the attention away from their attempts at matchmaking. "Peanut, what do you think about moving in here with Miss Petra?"

Munching on a potato chip, Peanut looked up at Raeder with wide eyes. "Can I bring Ralph?"

While June gave him a questioning look, Miss Petra guffawed. "Of course, you can bring Ralph. Wouldn't have it any other way."

June caught Raeder's gaze and mouthed, "Who's Ralph?"

He chewed his lip for a few seconds. "He's that stuffed giraffe Peanut carries just about anyplace. Haven't you noticed it at church? His mama made it for him when he was a baby." She'd worked on it during chemotherapy to keep her mind off her pain.

"Awww." June's blue eyes reddened, and she blinked like she was trying to keep some tears from putting in an appearance.

Raeder swallowed down his own emotions. Some memories of Audra stung more than others.

"A giraffe, eh?" Zeke seemed to think he had to put in his two cents. "You ever seen a giraffe in real life, Peanut?"

Brown eyes round with curiosity, Peanut shook his head.

"Then your daddy needs to take you up to the Rio Grande zoo in Albuquerque. They've got some mighty fine specimens. I read in the paper last week they got some new babies." Zeke chuckled. "Babies that're six feet tall." He swatted at Raeder's shoulder. "You gotta take him. Every kid needs to go to the zoo."

"Can we, Daddy?" Peanut bounced in his booster seat.

"Sure. One of these days. We got a rodeo to promote first."

"And Miss June can go with us?"

June blushed, and to Raeder's great annoyance, both Zeke and Miss Petra laughed like it was the funniest thing they'd ever heard.

Raeder glanced at his left wrist, where he used to wear a smart watch before it got smashed. "Would you look at the time. I got some alfalfa to cut. Y'all please excuse me." He stood and ruffled Peanut's hair. "You stay and help Miss Petra, okay?"

"Yessir." Bless his sweet heart, he was used to being shuffled around. Raeder didn't know what he'd do if he didn't have good friends to help him out.

He grabbed his old Stetson from the mudroom hat rack, then plopped it on his head and made a quick exit. Only time would bring an end to all this teasing about June and him. Time, and maybe her finding a cowboy worthy of her attention. As always, such thoughts brought an ache to his chest… until he reminded himself that she was always meddling in his parenting, not to mention she kept trying to change Peanut's name—the name his mother called him by. And Raeder planned to keep Audra alive in his son's mind, and his own heart, for as long as he could.

The visit with the New Mexico Barrel Racing Association folks in Albuquerque went even better than expected, with the board and attending members being enthusiastic about adding the stampede to their list of approved events. Being a NMBRA member herself, June did most of the talking, but she'd observed several of the ladies eyeing Raeder. And no wonder. He was one good-looking cowboy. As they drove back to Riverton, she couldn't resist teasing him.

"So did you notice that gal from Clovis? She sure had an eye for you. Did you get her number?"

Raeder glanced in the rearview mirror, probably to check on Peanut, asleep in his booster in the back seat. "Nope. But I did see that rancher on the committee checking you out. Did he ask for your number?"

June laughed. "Actually, he did…shortly before his wife came up and introduced herself."

Eyebrows raised, he shot her a look, then refocused on the road. "Huh. Some people…"

"I know. Before she came over, I asked him if he knew Jesus. He didn't seem to know how to answer that. I don't know whether his wife's arrival saved him or me."

Raeder chuckled. "Either way, looks like the Lord had it all timed out."

"As He always does." She liked the way his faith came through automatically when he talked about the Lord.

"I know Jesus," Peanut piped up from the back seat.

"Uh-oh." June winced, then looked back to see Peanut's sweet, trusting smile. "Yes, you do." She turned to Raeder. "Little pitchers have big ears. Sorry for teasing you." She'd always been careful with her words, and especially around little ones.

"No problem. On another subject, you still want to take Darby out for a ride?"

"Sure do. Tuesday okay with you?"

"Sounds good."

That weekend, when Raeder picked up RJ after Sunday school, it seemed natural for the three of them to walk together across the church campus to the sanctuary for the morning service. It felt natural for them to sit in the same pew. And when they shared a hymnbook, June was reminded of her plans to recommend Raeder's fine baritone voice to Wayne, the choir director, when choir started up again in the fall.

At the end of the service, when one of June's teens, Jeff Sizemore, suggested that Raeder and Peanut should go with the group for their usual pizza outing, June's silly heart did a little hop. What was wrong with her? She'd just spent an entire church service with the cowboy. Wasn't he getting tired of her company?

"What'd'ya think, Raeder?" Jeff said.

Raeder cast a doubtful glance at June. "Don't want to crash your party."

"Well," June drawled, trying to think of a reasonable way to say no despite liking the idea. Shouldn't she protect her time with her teens? "I don't know."

"Aw, come on, guys." Jeff tousled RJ's hair, then had a brief, playful sparring match with him. "I sure do miss this little pest." Jeff had lived at Miss Petra's ranch since last February and learned how to do ranch chores from Raeder. June suspected Jeff missed the dad as much as the son.

"Oh, okay." June pretended reluctance but couldn't hide a smile. "You'd better come with us, Raeder. Sometimes I need help to ride herd on these kids."

That wasn't far from the truth. Three years ago, June had started this Sunday tradition with two of her teen cousins and three of their friends. It had grown to include members of the youth group and whoever happened to attend the morning service. They were noisy and messy, but mostly they behaved themselves well enough.

Once they were all settled at the pizza parlor she enjoyed watching Raeder interact with her kids. The girls made it clear they liked his good looks and nice manners, and every one of them wanted to baby RJ. On the other hand, the guys wanted to talk with Raeder about bull riding and rodeo life in general. To his credit, he focused on each one in turn with grace. Maybe, like her, he'd learned to be so personable when crowds thronged him after his successful rodeo rides. Yet, unlike some bronco busters she'd met, he wasn't boastful or dismissive. He fit into the group as if he'd been hanging out with them for months.

After an hour of pizza, soda and noisy fellowship, little RJ, thumb in mouth, fell asleep in June's Cousin Mandy's arms.

"Thanks, Mandy." Raeder scooped him up. "Guess I'd better get him home."

Goodbyes were chorused by the group, which was ready to break up, anyway.

June walked Raeder to the restaurant door and held it open for him. "See you Tuesday?"

"Lookin' forward to it."

She watched him cross the parking lot, her heart warm with admiration for his love and care for his son. She shook herself. That little guy was so much more than a peanut. Maybe over these next few months as they promoted the rodeo, she could convince Raeder to call his son *RJ*, and maybe throw out a few hints from time to time. That was, if she could do it without getting on his nerves.

After Raeder finished feeding the cattle on Tuesday, did his other morning chores and tacked up Darby, he headed to the big house to clean up and get Peanut ready for their ride with June. Since his injury and subsequent road to recovery, he hadn't had the time or good health to travel around and see much of the area, so he looked forward to whatever her tour would include. She'd promised to bring lunch, one less thing for him to worry about. But if they traveled to a higher altitude, he'd need to bring a jacket for Peanut. Since his forced withdrawal from the rodeo circuit and settling in at Miss Petra's ranch, he'd been concentrating so much on healing that he'd forgotten all the little things required for travel with his son. This being a day trip, if he forgot something, they could probably manage for a few hours without it. Still, when he finished cleaning up and headed to the kitchen, he glanced around for anything he should take along for the day.

"What's got you all in a lather?" Miss Petra stood at her kitchen counter, Peanut watching at her elbow, using an ice-cream scoop to measure out chocolate-chip cookie dough onto a baking sheet.

"I'm not…" No use trying to fool his boss lady. "Just don't want to forget anything we might need." He tilted his head toward Peanut and searched for a diversion. "Ma'am, your kitchen always smells *sooo* good." He risked getting his hand swatted and pinched bites of the dough for himself and Peanut.

Instead, she grinned at Raeder in that teasing way of hers. "So are you looking forward to spending the day with June?"

Peanut was quick to answer. "Yes, ma'am." His face lit up.

Miss Petra winked at Raeder. "I'm sure both of you are."

Raeder scrambled for a way to end her matchmaking hints. "If you must know, I'm looking forward to riding Shadow again. I sure have missed him."

Miss Petra's expression sobered, and her eyes reddened. "Oh, Raeder, I'm so sorry you had to sell him. That must have broken your heart."

Always sensitive to the adults he was around, Peanut looked back and forth between her and Raeder, and his thumb went into his mouth.

"Hey, the Lord provided a fine new owner." Raeder forced a chuckle before his own emotions got the better of him. "Somebody who takes care of him as good as I did. Maybe even better, Eli being a vet and all."

Miss Petra seemed to catch on. "Yep. Yep. You can always count on the Lord." She tapped Peanut's nose. "And don't you forget it."

He giggled, that musical sound Raeder loved so much.

The blast of a truck horn from outside was another welcome sound.

"Let's go, buddy." Raeder grabbed his backpack with one hand and Peanut's hand with the other, while Peanut grabbed the plastic bag of cookies Miss Petra had made earlier. "Thanks for the cookies, ma'am. We'll be back before time for evening milking."

"Never you mind, son." She waved him off. "Jeff's driving now, so he can come over and do the milking. You have a good time and don't hurry back."

"Yes, ma'am." He hurried toward the door before she could offer any more matchmaking comments.

Outside, they approached June's red pickup.

Her usual sunny self, she hopped out smiling. "Hey, R… Peanut. Hey, Raeder."

There she went, almost calling Peanut RJ again. Not a good way for this day's outing to begin. And one more reason Miss Petra's matchmaking was pointless.

Peanut plunged into her open arms like they hadn't seen each other in a month instead of two days.

Raeder touched the brim of his hat. "Mornin', June. If you'll hang on to *Peanut*, I'll bring Darby out." Why had he let himself get talked into this? Easy answer. He and Peanut had very few breaks from routine, so he'd try to make it a fun day for his son, at least.

He loaded Darby into the trailer behind June's pickup, glad that Shadow greeted this stranger with a nicker instead of a snort. Darby was one of those easygoing horses all the others took to right away. After stroking Shadow's nose and whispering his own greeting to his old friend, Raeder fetched Peanut's booster from the Bronco and secured it in the pickup's back seat, then fastened Peanut in. The aroma of homemade fried chicken filled the cabin, along with the unmistakable scent of chocolate. Maybe this day would turn out all right after all, at least in the food department.

"Okay, guys, let's get this show on the road." June hopped into the driver's seat.

"I don't mind driving." Raeder stood outside the driver's-side door.

She gave a sharp shake of her head. "I've got this." She grinned in her cute, smarty-pants way. "I should probably blindfold you so our destination will be a surprise 'til we get there."

"Uh, that's a no." He chuckled as he rounded the truck to the passenger side. Yeah, this day would be fine…as long as she didn't start meddling with Peanut's name again.

Instead, she started singing. "Jesus loves me, this I know…" By the time she reached the second line, Peanut had joined in, so Raeder added his voice to make it a trio. When they finished, she cast one of her teacher looks at Raeder. "That does it. You're joining the church choir this fall."

"What?" He laughed. "I've never sung in a choir."

"You haven't?" She cast him another look, this one doubtful. "But you harmonize so well."

He shrugged. "My ma used to sing with us kids at the piano." When Pa wasn't around. But he wouldn't mention that part to June. With her perfect, loving family, especially her pa, he doubted she'd understand.

After the bumpy drive up the lane to the highway, they headed toward town, took the bypass, then kept on going. With the Sangre de Cristo Mountains visible in the distance to the north, he wondered if she meant to go that far.

After another ten minutes, they turned off the highway and approached a massive arched redbrick entrance with a wrought-iron name emblazoned across it—Double Bar M Ranch. June pulled up next to a gatepost and punched in a code, and the iron gate swung inward.

"Hey, I thought we were going down to the river." Raeder

surveyed the vast property in front of them. He'd wanted to see the original Mattson ranch where the family's New Mexico story began for a long time but wouldn't say that to June. He'd seen dozens of huge spreads in his rodeo days, when wealthy folks would invite him for a meal after a successful ride. He'd even dreamed of eventually having his own place, bought with rodeo winnings. That dream died last October when ol' Spite and Malice came down hard on Raeder's left knee.

"Patience, cowboy." She laughed. "We'll get there."

The truck and horse trailer lumbered across the iron cattle guard just inside the gate. On the right, a small herd of Angus cattle grazed in a pasture. Ahead on the left stood a massive white antebellum-style mansion. June nodded toward it.

"That's the original Mattson house, built by my great-great-grandparents in the 1880s. Rob and his family live there now." She pointed to a smaller but still big two-story house on the right. "That's Andy and Linda's house." Andy Mattson was the foreman of the Double Bar M Ranch, working for his cousin Rob Mattson, the family's Big Boss. "And over there—" She nodded toward a one-story pink adobe structure. "Sam and Juliet just moved in there. And, of course, Jeff and Sassy." She eyed Raeder. "I'm sure you miss them."

"I miss them," Peanut piped up from the back seat.

"Me, too, buddy." Raeder glanced over his shoulder. "Hey, look at the calves over there."

The diversion worked. Peanut giggled at the antics of the younger calves scampering around the pasture.

June drove past the houses and pulled up next to a humongous red barn. "We can unload here, then ride down to the river."

She pointed beyond a lower pasture toward the now-visible Rio Grande some one hundred yards away. Protecting the pasture from the usual summer flood waters was a twenty-foot levee, with the numerous cottonwood, pinion, juniper and ponderosa pines creating a small forest.

Raeder had to admire the way June had packed their picnic in saddlebags, along with fishing poles in leather cases. To his surprise, she was also packing a handgun, which she tucked away in one of the saddlebags.

"You think we need that?"

"Probably not. But you never can tell when a varmint will get curious and want to join us."

"I suppose." He sometimes carried a gun around Miss Petra's ranch but so far hadn't had to use it.

"You ride Shadow," she said. "I want to see how Darby's doing. And I should have Peanut with me since he's used to Darby. Okay?"

Raeder eyed her briefly. "Peanut'll ride with me. Shadow's good with him, too."

"Oh." She blinked those pretty blue eyes like he'd spoken in a language she didn't understand. "Well…"

"I can take turns." Peanut looked back and forth between them, a hint of worry scrunching his forehead.

"Sure, buddy. Good idea." Raeder lifted him up onto Shadow's saddle, where he'd had his first ride at eighteen months old, then climbed up behind his son. "Ready?"

"Ready." Peanut leaned back against him, his cowboy hat tilted to the side, fully confident in his daddy's ability to protect him.

But while he could protect his son on horseback, could he protect him from a meddling woman?

Chapter Six

June had promised herself she wouldn't let her preferred name for RJ slip out, but she had trouble calling him Peanut. She'd never tried to intrude in the raising of other people's kids other than to report any problems she saw in her Sunday school class, which were few. Even little Tessa didn't tease him again about her peanut allergy. Still, June wanted the precious boy to grow up with a positive self-esteem, as she did all her students.

She'd seen the hurt an unusual nickname could cause a child. With an almost dismissive nickname like Peanut, how would he regard himself? She could just imagine the teasing he'd receive in middle school. What if he played high school sports? *Peanut just made another touchdown! Peanut set a new 400-meter dash record!* That might bring more laughter than cheers. Never mind the puns announcers would come up with.

Oh, well. It was clear Raeder wasn't interested in her thoughts on the matter, so all she could do was reinforce what a dear, smart boy he was in the short time she still had him in her class. And bite her tongue when she almost slipped out with RJ. *And* try to make this an enjoyable day for all of them.

"Okay, cowboys, follow me." She nudged Darby past the barn and toward her favorite trail beside the river.

Glancing back, she saw pure happiness on Raeder's handsome face as he held RJ with one arm and the reins with the other hand, while RJ held on to the saddle horn. Bringing Shadow for him to ride had been Dad's suggestion, one she'd quickly approved of. Raeder's relationship with the stallion was as dear to him as hers was with Sprinter. After today, she hoped he would accept her invitation to ride Shadow whenever he wanted.

She led them past a hundred-year-old cottonwood. "My brother, Eric, taught me to climb that tree when I was nine." She waved a hand at the giant tree.

Raeder looked over the thick, spreading branches and nodded his approval. "That's what big brothers are for."

"That's right." These days, Eric's lessons for her mostly involved showing her how to face his disability with courage. She shook off the sad thought. "You must be the big brother in your family."

When he didn't answer right away, she looked back again. From his guarded expression, he seemed to be considering how to answer. At last he gave a brief nod.

"Yep. Oldest of five."

"Oh, wow." She'd often wished for more siblings, but Mom's endometriosis had put an end to her parents' dream of a big family. "Brothers and sisters?"

"Two other boys, two girls."

"You must have had lots of fun growing up. You'll have to tell me all about them."

"We'll see."

Uh-oh. Sensitive subject. Better find a safe topic. She pointed to the massive growth of bushes up ahead, the branches thick with dark red ripening fruit. "Those are chokecherries. You probably know that. They produce a huge crop of berries every year. The Mattson teens pick them, and we ladies have a big canning party. We make enough jelly to feed the entire Mattson clan for a year."

"Not sure I believe that, June." To her relief, his tone was light and teasing. "That's a lot of Mattsons to feed."

"Yep. There's a lot of us. I'm not even sure how many."

"Now, that's funny." He laughed out loud, and RJ copied him, his sweet, high giggle warming June's heart. "Maybe you should make a chart." He nodded toward the bushes. "You do know chokecherry bushes can be fatal to livestock, right?"

"Sure do." She swatted at the flies trying to settle on Darby's head. "That's why we have that barbed-wire fencing along the lower pasture."

"Very good. I didn't notice that."

"I'm not surprised. There's lots to see here. Let's ride up onto the levee so we can get a good look at the river. I know a nice spot up there for our picnic."

"I'm hungry, Daddy," RJ said in a stage whisper to Raeder.

He chuckled and whispered back, "Me, too, buddy."

Listening to their interaction, June felt a little twinge near her heart. Raeder was such a good, caring father, and the two of them were such a sweet little family. Maybe someday in the future, the Lord would give her a family of her own—a husband and precious children.

Raeder dismounted and lifted Peanut down, then held on to the saddle while flexing his left leg. If he didn't keep up the exercises that worked out the kinks, the doc warned the scar tissue could grow together and make it impossible to bend the knee. Then, without another surgery, he'd be crippled for the rest of his life.

"Want to help me set out our picnic?" June had already taken down the saddlebags.

"I want to help." Peanut hopped over to June.

The warmth in her smile at his little boy always brought a happy feeling to Raeder's heart. But the feeling in his leg wasn't quite so pleasant right now.

"Do you mind watching Peanut for a bit while I walk down to the river's edge?" He gave her an apologetic grimace. "This bum leg of mine needs a little exercise after riding so long, and it helps to walk up and down." He chuckled to lighten his tone.

"Sure. Go ahead." She gave him a sympathetic frown. "Peanut and I can manage the food. Just don't take too long or we'll eat it all." Now, she was grinning.

"I'll make it quick."

The walk down the levee path caused more pain that he'd expected. For the first time in weeks, he wished for his cane. Walking back up was even worse. No surprise that when he got back to Peanut and June, he had worked up a sweat and increased his appetite, not to mention having to catch his breath.

June had laid out an orange-and-brown woolen blanket for them to sit on. She passed him a moist towelette and used one to clean up Peanut. "Raeder, will you please bless the food?" Her sweet smile made his heart stutter.

"I can bless the food." Peanut looked up at Raeder. "Can I, Daddy?"

"Sure thing, buddy."

"Y'all, please bow your heads."

Raeder had to swallow hard not to chuckle with joy over his son's precious earnestness. A quick look at June showed she was having the same struggle.

"Dear Jesus, thank You for the food and for the day and

for the ride on Shadow—we miss him so much—and for Miss June and for my daddy and for the birds and for the river and for the sun and the sky and this nice day. In Jesus's name, amen."

"Amen," Raeder and June chorused. The twinkle in her eyes revealed she was as blessed by Peanut's sweet prayer as he was. As for his mention of missing Shadow, Raeder forced down the pain that evoked. If the Lord wanted him to own the horse again, He'd have to provide a way Raeder couldn't begin to imagine. If not, it wasn't His will.

"Just finger food today." June set out paper plates, then passed around chicken drumsticks, potato chips, pickles and carrot sticks. "And plenty of wet wipes."

They ate for several minutes, quiet except for comments on how good everything was and hums of agreement.

"Darby's doing real well," June said at last. "I think you can start lining up students anytime now."

"That's good news." With his pay for being the poster cowboy for the rodeo, he wasn't feeling a financial pinch quite so bad these days, but that gig would end after the stampede in October. If he could win or even place in the bull riding, he'd have some money to start rebuilding his savings so he could buy his own place someday…if that wasn't too much to hope for.

He watched Shadow munching on some grass nearby, and his heart dipped. When he bought the registered stallion four years ago, he'd planned to use him for breeding. That dream died when his hospital bills and physical therapy ate up all of his insurance and savings, and he'd had to sell Shadow. With all of his own health bills, he didn't have anything left for regular vet visits, much less the insurance every responsible owner carried for their horses. But selling Shadow was more than the loss of his dream. He'd raised him from a yearling, and they'd bonded in a special way. Even today, it was like old times to ride him. When they headed back home, maybe he'd ask June to take Peanut on Darby so he could take Shadow for an all-out run. Did the horse even get that kind of exercise? Not something he could ask June, and especially not her pa. Then again, he thought, of course, Eli would do the best for his animals.

"I'd love to hear more about your brothers and sisters."

Her comment startled him from his thoughts. He'd rarely talked about family to his pals on the rodeo circuit. He looked at Peanut, who'd fallen asleep on the blanket, thumb in mouth. Maybe it wouldn't hurt to talk about his growing-up years. Once she heard about how different their lives had been, she'd pay no attention to the matchmaking Miss Petra and the others were trying to do. Not that she'd shown any real interest in him. Despite her suggesting their outing today, she was just doing her professional duty to evaluate Darby's fitness for lessons.

"Okay. What do you want to know?"

She gazed off toward the river for a moment. "Hmm. How about birth order?"

"Okay. Me first. Ally next. Colin next. Giselle next. And Elliott bringing up the rear. Spaced out about two or three years apart."

"I'm guessing they all looked up to you."

To avoid her intense gaze, he stared down at his greasy hands and grabbed another wet wipe. "I suppose."

"How about your folks? What do they do?"

This was the part where he had to be careful, especially with Peanut close by. Even asleep, he might hear something he shouldn't.

"They've got a small spread up in Wyoming. Not big, but okay for their needs. Ma stayed home to homeschool us. Now that Elliott's enrolled in high school so he could go out for football, Ma works in Douglas as a legal secretary."

"So your dad runs the ranch? Did he teach you—"

"No!" That came out too forcefully. "Sorry. I just don't talk about him."

"No, I'm sorry. I didn't mean to pry." Yet she still looked at him as if she was expecting more.

He shook his head. "That's okay." He released a long sigh as a familiar ache formed in his chest. "Pa was—" He glanced at Peanut, whose even breathing and relaxed thumb showed him in deep sleep. "He wasn't what you'd call a personable man. Never could please him."

June's eyes got a little red, but she pasted on her warm, full-face smile. "You said you sang with your mom. Tell me about that."

"Most evenings, she'd call us to gather 'round the piano and sing hymns. Giselle has a real fine voice and got a music scholarship for college this fall." He chuckled. "The rest of us manage to croak along to the music."

"Ha. Remember, I've heard you sing. I'll bet you miss those family sing-alongs. You ought to get a guitar and learn to accompany yourself." She reached down and touched Peanut's curly hair. "You owe it to him to give him a musical experience like you had."

"Not a bad idea." No use telling her he had a guitar he hadn't played in a while. Maybe after he had a chance to practice, he'd surprise her with a serenade. Well, not a serenade. She might get the wrong idea. Just a song. "Maybe he'd like to join the kids' choir at church this fall."

Her smile showed she liked that idea.

"Now, it's your turn. Tell me about growing up Mattson." She rolled her eyes. "If I must."

"Hey, fair is fair."

"Right." She shrugged. "For one thing, everybody in town and most of the state is always nice to us just because of our name, even those of us who didn't grow up on the Double Bar M."

Raeder stifled a chuckle, forced a frown and shook his head. "What a terrible way to grow up."

She burst out with a laugh so loud Peanut bolted awake.

"What's so funny?" He sat up and rubbed his eyes.

Which only made June laugh harder. Raeder felt the tension in his chest loosen, and he laughed, too. June sure was a good sport. And if she thought people were nice to her because she was a Mattson, she was downright mistaken. Other than her pestering ways about Peanut's name and schooling, she was just about the nicest young lady he'd ever known. Too bad she was too far above him socially for him to explore a deeper relationship. She'd probably end up marrying money. Besides, he and Peanut had a good thing going at Miss Petra's ranch. No use messing it up by getting interested in a woman.

Shadow snorted noisily, the sound resonating into a rumble from his throat. Raeder could see him straining against his lead, which was loosely tied to a low-hanging tree branch. At the sight of a rattlesnake slithering across the top of the levee some eight yards away, Raeder carefully rose to his feet, once again having to work out the kink in his bum knee.

"Peanut, stay with Miss June." Raeder walked slowly toward Shadow. "Easy, boy. It's okay. Shh—shh."

Darby glanced up from his grazing but didn't seem bothered by the snake, probably because he was one of those older horses who'd seen and heard just about everything and had learned to be bomb-proof. Raeder grasped Shadow's reins and secured the lead to the branch, then looked back at June.

Not surprisingly, she had pulled her pistol from the saddlebag and was whispering to Peanut.

"We don't want to harm him unless he threatens us," she said to his son in a calm, smooth tone. "He's more scared of us than we are of him. If he comes this way, we can warn him off with a shot just like he would warn us with his rattles if we got too close to him. We don't want to hit him because he gets rid of mice and other small pests on the ranch."

Peanut nodded, his expression serious. Raeder heaved out a long breath as his admiration for June exploded. He'd always been the one to protect his son, but she hadn't even blinked at taking on the challenge. And her steady, unflappable nature sure was more than impressive. Like Darby, she seemed to be bomb-proof.

After a moment the snake slithered away, no doubt in search of some hapless field mouse or gecko or other favored critter on his menu. Steadying himself, Raeder ambled back to the blanket, wanting to gather his son in his arms and ride away. Then again, he thought, maybe the Lord had sent that rattler for a reason. So Peanut could learn to be cautious but not scared of danger by watching his dad and June react calmly. Now, if the Almighty would just help Raeder learn not to be too interested in a woman who never ceased to surprise him.

June drew in deep, quiet breaths, glad that she'd managed not to tremble at the sight of the rattler. She'd learned early in working with her younger cousins and later as she began to teach Sunday school not to panic or let her emotions get away from her. In truth, she hated snakes and would gladly have dispatched that one with a single shot, had RJ not been in her care.

She gave Raeder a big smile when he returned to their

picnic blanket. They'd made a good team just now in the same way they did when they were out on their rodeo junkets. But for RJ's sake, she wouldn't mention the snake again. Instead, she pointed to her khaki canvas fishing-pole holder still hanging from Darby's saddle. "Ready to catch some trout?"

As always, Raeder understood her diversion. "Sure. The river seems a little high and fast for fishing, but I'm game if you are."

"You're right. It's pretty high. But I know a great fishing spot on Mattson Creek, a feeder stream over there." She pointed beyond the trees in the opposite direction from the snake's path.

"Let's go." He helped her pack up the picnic. "You're gonna learn to catch fish, buddy."

The little guy grinned, trust in his dad beaming from his eyes. "Gonna catch fish!"

Twenty minutes later, they'd relocated to a shady spot beside the flowing stream that bordered the ranch's lower pasture. Raeder helped June unpack the three rods and assemble them.

"Aw, that's cute." He held up the child-size rod with its fully functional reel. "Did you learn to fish with this one?"

"Sure did." She longed to show RJ how to use it, but maybe it was best if his dad did the honors. "Go ahead." She nodded toward the boy, whose adorable face was lit up with excitement. "Show him how it's done." She handed him the can of worms she'd purchased at the feed store.

"Cool. You brought bait." He opened the can. "I was thinking we'd have to dig for worms."

"We could do that instead if you want to teach Peanut how." Not her favorite thing to do, but she could go with the flow.

"No need. They're probably down pretty deep, this being the heat of the day." He dug a fat, squirming worm out of the can. "Okay, son, here's what you do." He attached the bait to the hook. "Now, when you cast out your line, always be aware of where the hook goes. You don't want to snag it on a bush."

"Or a person." June hadn't meant to say that out loud. She mouthed "sorry" to Raeder.

"No, you're right." He grinned. "Definitely don't want to hook a person."

She had to look away. If he didn't want to hook a person, he really shouldn't smile at her in that cute cowboy way of his. Did he even know what his grin could do to a girl's heart? Not hers, of course. She'd known cute cowboys all her life without it causing her any trouble. But she sure could see the appeal in this one. His lack of awareness about his looks only made him more attractive.

They settled down to quiet fishing, with Raeder whispering instructions to RJ while neglecting his own rod, which he'd propped up on rocks and driftwood, its line flowing with the stream toward the river. A tiny bounce of the pole hinted he might have a fish nibbling at his bait, so she edged closer. Sure enough, the pole started to move sharply toward the fast-flowing stream.

"You've got a bite!" She dropped her own rod and grabbed his before it hit the water and held tight. "Want to reel it in?"

"No, you go ahead."

Good man. He wouldn't leave his little boy's side even to catch a fish.

She waited until just the right moment, like her big brother had taught her years ago, then yanked the rod to set the hook. A medium-size trout jumped out of the water, fighting against the line.

"You got him!" Raeder swayed in her direction, clearly wishing to offer help, which she didn't need. "Now, reel him in nice and steady so he doesn't slip away."

"You stick to helping RJ… Peanut, I mean." She really must stop doing that. "He's the one who needs your help." She tilted her head to RJ's bouncing bobber.

If she hadn't been looking, she would have missed Raeder's scowl. Way to ruin a nice day, she chided herself.

She removed the slippery trout from the hook and dropped it into her wicker creel. "Looks like you've got one, too, Peanut." If she amended her words, maybe Raeder would forget her earlier goof.

Father and son fought the fish for several minutes, finally landing it onto the grassy creek bank.

"I got a fish! I got a fish!" Clapping his hands, RJ hopped around while the fish flopped back toward the water.

"Hang on, buddy." Raeder still held the pole. "Job's not done 'til he's in the creel."

Well away from the water, he showed RJ how to unhook the flopping fish. June held out the creel so he could drop his catch through the square hole in the top.

"Way to go, guys," June cheered as the father and son shared a high five.

Another half hour resulted in two more fish, one for Raeder and another for RJ…with his dad's help.

"Guess I better get back to the ranch." Raeder started detaching the reel and dismantling his rod. "Those cows won't milk themselves."

"Miss Petra said Jeffie could do the milking." RJ blinked his brown eyes. "I want to catch more fish."

"Maybe another day." Raeder kept packing.

Lower lip jutted out, RJ plopped down on the grass and crossed his arms. "I want to fish."

Raeder blinked, and his jaw went slack.

"Maybe we could go get ice cr—" June began.

"No." Raeder waved a hand to stop her. "No rewards for disobedience." He kneeled beside RJ. "Son, it's time to go. Get up now and brush off." His tone was soft but firm.

Pout still in place, RJ eyed him, then smiled at June. "Can we stay and fish?"

"You don't ask her, Peanut. You mind me."

Big tears formed in RJ's eyes. "Awww-right." He heaved out a huge sigh, got to his feet and brushed the seat of his jeans.

June thought her heart would melt. Raeder was right, of course, but she often took the easy or playful route with other people's kids. How would she react if the Lord ever blessed her with her own child? Her admiration for Raeder rose a few notches. If he wasn't bound and determined to ride the bulls again—and possibly leave this precious boy an orphan—she might be tempted to let herself be interested in him. But that was a deal-breaker. She wouldn't let go of her heart no matter how appealing this cowboy was.

Chapter Seven

Around seven o'clock, with the sun still hanging above the horizon, Raeder settled Peanut on a blanket in Riverton Park to watch the Independence Day concert in the amphitheater down the hill. He'd always taught his son they needed to be thankful they lived in a free country, and tonight's patriotic music and speeches should reinforce those lessons.

Too bad he couldn't introduce him to fireworks, but apparently the city couldn't pull that off, maybe due to the expense. Instead, the city announced they would end this evening's entertainment here at the amphitheater with a video on the giant outdoor screen of fireworks from Washington, DC, and the National Symphony Orchestra accompanying the colorful explosions.

Today, after Raeder completed the usual chores around Miss Petra's ranch, they'd spent an hour or so chasing after Peanut's chickens, who weren't ready to be penned up in their safe coop before sundown. When the last hen had finally been caught, they headed out to the park for a rare evening of entertainment away from home. And since moving into the big house, the ranch did seem like home. As he often did, Raeder lifted a silent prayer of thanks for God's goodness in providing a stable place for him to raise Peanut. The ranch might not be his, but the way Miss Petra welcomed them both into her heart, it was the next best place where they could live until he could save enough money for his own land.

Some fifty feet away, he saw June arriving with her family. He'd briefly met her brother, Eric, the day they'd shot their publicity photos for the rodeo promotions. Eric hadn't been well, so Raeder hadn't hung around to get further acquainted. This evening, as they lowered their van lift holding his wheelchair, Eric appeared much better, at least from this distance. Maybe he should pack up Peanut and join them.

Before he could move, he saw a passel of Mattsons gather around them and decided it was a larger family affair. Best not to intrude. Yet he felt a sharp pang in his chest. Growing up, he'd always spent Independence Day and other holidays with his own family. He missed the camaraderie he'd enjoyed with Ma and his siblings. What were they doing tonight? Did his brothers and sisters make sure Ma had a good time? She loved fireworks. Did they take her out to a live show?

"Daddy, I'm hungry." Peanut eyed the bag of hot dogs and fries Raeder had bought from one of the food trucks parked around the perimeter of the city grounds.

"Me, too, buddy." Raeder pulled out a disposable plastic bib from his jeans pocket. "Here you go."

Peanut pushed against his hand. "I don't want that."

Raeder paused. Was this disobedience or wanting to be more grown up? "Well, how about you do me a favor and wear it anyway. It's not easy for me to wash the mustard out of your T-shirts."

Peanut mulled that over for a few seconds, his smooth forehead wrinkled thoughtfully. Then he sighed. "Ooo-kay."

He rolled his eyes in resignation while Raeder bit his lip to hide a smile. Having always been agreeable in most situations, his son was becoming more of his own person.

How'm I doin', Audra?

Before she died, she'd prayed he'd be a wise single father once she had to leave them, but he often doubted himself. It didn't help when June kept calling Peanut *RJ*, even though he had to admit that was kinda cute. No, it would only confuse Peanut, and he'd had enough confusion in his young life with all the frequent changes. As for her disapproval of his determination to return to bull riding for fear he'd leave Peanut an orphan, she needn't worry. He had no doubt his sister Ally would gladly take her nephew in. Even though she was two years younger than Raeder, she'd been a second mother to all her siblings, and she'd offered to help with Peanut after Audra died. 'Course, it probably would be a good idea to remind Ally of that and see if she wanted to make it official. He hadn't called or emailed anybody back home since leaving four years ago. Hadn't logged on to his laptop in months, either. Maybe he should dust it off and see if Miss Petra had Wi-Fi. But then, maybe an out-of-the-blue email to his sister probably wasn't the best way to ask such an important question as raising someone else's child. He'd have to pray about it some more before he did anything.

"Hey, cowboy." June snuck up on him looking her usual gorgeous self, and he almost dropped his hot dog. She was all decked out in one of her rodeo-queen outfits—white Western-cut suit, white-and-gold Miss Riverton Stampede sash, hat with its silver-and-gold crown hatband and rhinestone-studded white boots. Every time he saw her in her fancy queen getup, he felt a jolt. She was movie-star beautiful, no doubt about it.

He gulped down his bite of hot dog. "Hey, yourself."

"Miss June!" Peanut hopped up and started for her.

"Hold on, buddy." Raeder barely had time to catch him one-handed. "Let's don't get mustard on her fancy outfit."

To her credit, she didn't cringe away from Peanut, just

reached out a hand to shake his…and to keep him at a distance for the safety of her fine clothes. "Howdy, cowboy."

"Howdy!" Peanut shook her hand and giggled, that musical sound Raeder loved to hear.

"So I know you're probably sick of seeing me since we're together almost every weekend." She sighed wearily, though he could see the teasing glint in her pretty blue eyes. "But the family insisted that I come over and invite you to join us."

Raeder laughed. "Well, ma'am, sounds to me like you're the one sick of seeing *me*. But me and Peanut might do you a favor so you don't get in trouble with your folks. We'll come over for a bit. What do you say, pardner?" He nudged Peanut.

"Yeah! I wanna go see Sassy." Hot dog still in one hand, he dashed away.

"Peanut, wait!" Raeder lunged for him but missed. "Come back here."

"I'll watch him." June laughed. "You pack up and come on over when you're ready." She sashayed away, waving to folks who tried to stop her for a chat or a picture. "Sorry, y'all. Got a boy to catch." She broke into a trot to back up her claim.

Raeder shook his head as he gathered his blanket and bag of food to follow them. He appreciated the way she hadn't been distracted from catching his son even for the short fifty-foot walk to join her family. No doubt about it. June Mattson was good people, as all her folks seemed to be. Good *wealthy* people, he reminded himself. Far too wealthy for the likes of him. He mentally shrugged. So what? Over his nine years of participating in the rodeo world, he'd rubbed shoulders with some of the wealthiest ranchers in the US, lots of them with pretty daughters. Why would his interactions with the Mattsons be any different?

Eli, Sue and Eric greeted him like an old friend, as did the others, and he exchanged the usual pleasantries with them, all the while checking on Peanut, who was having the time of his life chasing around with Sassy and a couple of her smaller cousins. Then Raeder looked for a place to lay out his blanket.

"Right here, Raeder." Eric waved a hand to the grassy spot beside his wheelchair. "Time for us to get acquainted."

Uh-oh. Did he want to talk rodeo stuff or interrogate Raeder about all the time he spent with his sister? Either way, he had no choice but to settle on the blanket at an angle where he could both watch Peanut and chat with this former bull rider…hopefully without getting a crick in his neck.

"This should be a pretty good concert." Eric nodded toward the small amphitheater down the hill. "Local musicians but talented. A couple of them could do well in Nashville."

"That so?" Raeder had his musical preferences, and if these folks were Nashville-worthy, he wouldn't have to endure any opera-style warbling.

"How're you doing, Raeder?" Keen interest shone in Eric's eyes, which were as blue as June's. "Getting healed up okay?"

"Pretty much. Still have a few kinks to work out."

"I can imagine…or should I say remember?" Eric chuckled. "Before my last ride, I had the usual broken bones and stuff but never torn ligaments. But pain is pain, right?"

In the waning daylight, Raeder searched Eric's face for any sign of self-pity so he'd know how to answer. Sure, he'd felt a lot of pain. It was part of being a bull rider. But despite his limp, which was slowly dissipating, he could still walk, unlike Eric, who according to June was bound to that chair for the rest of his life. Yet Raeder saw only intense interest in the other man's question.

"Yep. Pain is part of the package in our sport." Should he have said "our"?

"Don't I know it." Eric chuckled. "When do you plan to ride again?"

Not *if*, but *when*. Raeder grinned, knowing he'd found a kindred spirit.

"October."

Eric nodded. "The Riverton Stampede. I'll be praying for you. And watching. And wishing I could be competing against you." No regret or self-pity, just a simple statement salted with cowboy humor.

Raeder grinned. "Me, too." He glanced beyond his new-found friend to where June was watching them, an uncharacteristic frown marring her pretty face. No need to wonder what she was thinking.

The squeals and laughter from the children caught their attention. In place of Fourth of July sparklers, somebody had brought along some fancy bubble toys, and Peanut was in the thick of it, trying to catch the soapy orbs along with the other kids. Raeder's heart warmed to see his son getting along so well with the Mattson kids. If he hadn't already planned to homeschool him, he could have rested easy if Peanut had to go to public school, knowing he'd have ready-made friends. Not for the first time, he briefly second-guessed a major decision about the way he was raising his son. No, he'd already lost Audra. He wasn't ready to lose Peanut to influences beyond his control, so they'd be homeschooling, no matter what June thought about it.

June barely had time to process the disturbing conversation she'd overheard between her brother and her promotional partner. No, he was more than that. He was RJ's dad, responsible in every way except when it came to bull riding, the very sport that had put Eric in that chair.

"Ready, Miss Riverton Stampede?" Everly Strait hustled over to her family group. "Let's get up on that stage."

June forced a smile. "Yessir. Let's go." She followed Everly down the slope to the amphitheater.

Once he got the mic situated so it didn't squeal, he welcomed everybody, then invited June to give her usual speech about the Riverton Stampede. The crowd of a thousand or more people responded with cheers. She hoped those cheers translated into attendance in October. Meanwhile, her job was to keep the fires of interest burning 'til then.

Pastor Tim gave the invocation, with thanks for the blessings of freedom. Zeke Baldwin recited parts of the Declaration of Independence from memory. Then Casey Spellman, a high-school senior, sang the national anthem a cappella, with the crowd enthusiastically joining in. Next came the high school bluegrass ensemble with their lively music and true-blue country singing. Four or five more acts were to follow.

Her duty done, June returned to her pickup, made a quick change into jeans and a red T-shirt, stowed her queen regalia and then joined her family. Now, where should she sit? Newlyweds Sam and Juliet sat with their daughter, Sassy, and Juliet's brother, Jeff. Cousin Rob and Lauren had brought canvas chairs for themselves and their newly blended family of four children. Likewise Cousin Will and Olivia sat with their three kids—including their new baby girl—and their five foster boys. They'd settled near the exit so they could make a quick getaway if the children got unruly.

That left her own folks, and Raeder, of course, and she was quickly reminded of his earlier conversation with Eric. Maybe it'd been a bad idea to get those two together. For some reason she would never be able to fathom, her brother still loved bull riding. And now, he would only be an encouragement to Raeder to go back to that sport when he should be concentrating on taking care of his son and ensuring his future.

"Hey, sis!" Eric beckoned to her. "You're missing some good music."

She pasted on a smile, ambled over to him and plopped down on Raeder's blanket. RJ crawled out of his dad's arms and nestled up against her. As before, her heart melted. Did RJ cling to her because he needed a mom? She didn't mind being a womanly influence in his life as long as he was in her Sunday school class. But for some reason, she feared she would miss him a lot more than any of her graduating students when he moved up to the kindergarten class in late August and when she and Raeder completed their promotional work for the rodeo.

"You're listening to 95.3 KYDN, your hot sizzling country sound for radio and online in the San Luis Valley and beyond. This is Jack T reminding you to get your tickets for the Ski Hi Stampede, Colorado's oldest pro rodeo, coming up this Thursday through Sunday. There's something for everyone at the San Luis Valley's own Ski Hi Stampede! You won't want to miss any of the events, from the daily parades going right down Main Street to the carnival with all its brand-new rides at the fairgrounds to the biggest event, the rodeo at the San Luis Valley arena at the Ski Hi Complex in Monte Vista. Come on out and watch your favorite cowboys and cowgirls compete in their best events for some mighty impressive cash prizes. Tickets available online or at the ticket office. Y'all come on out! Now, here's Jelly Roll with his latest hit." A soulful guitar intro, followed by the award-winning country singer's unmistakable clear and melodious voice, filled the cabin of June's pickup.

This time Raeder was driving as they headed north, hauling Sprinter and Shadow in the horse trailer. He couldn't help feeling a little jealous of June. Not only did she get to participate in the queen activities, but she'd also be competing in the barrel racing. While both of them would ride in the daily parades with the Riverton Stampede banner strung between their horses, his own competitive nature made him want to try his skill on one of those bulls this rodeo was famous for. But his practices on the mechanical bull at Raintree Restaurant, even with Cody Martinez's coaching, needed more work before he could participate in the real thing. And he sure didn't want to mess up his big return to the Riverton arena in October.

"Have you checked your competition out?" He glanced at June, who was staring out the passenger window. "The other barrel racers?"

"Yeah, I did check the roster. I've ridden against most of the girls and should do pretty well." She chuckled. "Or at least not embarrass myself."

"I should hope not. You rode real good at Santa Fe. Do you have a trainer?" Guilt pinched at his conscience. Why hadn't he asked her that before? Sometimes he focused so much on his own stuff he forgot to show interest in other people.

"Just my dad and mom. Mom did a bit of barrel racing in her day, so she watches me practice in our home arena and gives me tips."

"Don't you think you'd do better with a professional coach?" Surely, the Mattsons could afford one, especially after buying an expensive registered quarter horse like Sprinter so she could participate in these rodeos.

"We do okay."

He glanced her way again. "You don't sound too excited."

She shrugged. "I do enjoy it." A brief laugh. "As the event comes closer, I usually feel sort of ambivalent." A bigger laugh. "Then I get on Sprinter and hear my name called, and *bang*! You can't hold me back. I want to win for all I'm worth *and* beat my previous time. I mean, if I'm gonna do it, I should give it my best, right?"

He joined her laughter. "That's real funny."

"You think? What about you? When you were competing, how did you feel right before your ride?"

"Oh, I go all out all the time. I practice mentally and physically so I can stay on that bull for my full eight seconds and hope he gives me a ride worthy of the top score."

"I'm sure you'll always miss it." Her voice held a hint of certainty, as if he'd given up his sport.

Time to set her straight on that. "Sure will…when I actually retire."

"But—"

"Daddy, what's *retire*?" Peanut, now awake from his nap in the back seat, reminded Raeder he needed to be careful with his words.

"That's when somebody quits doing something they've done for a long time."

June laughed and groaned at the same time. "That's one way to say it."

"Hey, you're the teacher. You tell him what *retire* means."

She pulled out her cell phone and punched it. "Okay, here's what the dictionary says. 'To withdraw from action or danger.' Danger. Hmm. Sounds appropriate for you and bull—"

"Nope. Don't go there. I'm not quitting anytime soon."

She released a little growl and turned back to the passenger window.

That was fine with Raeder. He got that she was concerned about Peanut, and that was all well and good. But she needed to quit hinting he should stop the one thing that gave him a chance to redeem himself, prove himself, if only *to* himself.

It was like Pa's voice in his head all over again saying he was a loser and nothing he did would ever amount to anything. He was having a hard enough time shutting down these self-doubts. He didn't need June's discouraging words to add to his struggles.

June couldn't regret her hints to Raeder, but maybe it was time to stop talking to him and just keep talking to the Lord about it. She watched the beautiful scenery passing by—the San Luis Valley had been an inland sea in ancient times and was bordered by the Sangre de Cristo Mountains on the east and the San Juan range on the west. The valley's mostly flat topography was vastly different from the hill country around Riverton, but the Rio Grande's headwaters flowed from the San Juans, through this area and down to Riverton, connecting the two locations. And, of course, the two areas shared a Wild West heritage. Raeder and June turned west in Alamosa and drove toward Monte Vista, home of the historic Ski Hi Stampede.

After checking in at the Ski Hi Complex in the late afternoon, parking the trailer and securing their horses in their assigned stalls, they drove the pickup to the Monte Villa Hotel in downtown Monte Vista. The hotel was abuzz with folks in town for the rodeo, and it took some time to get registered. After leaving their luggage in their respective rooms, they returned to the lobby to socialize. They'd arranged for a meeting with some of the Ski Hi Stampede planning committee to discuss the details of their appearances at the various events.

June greeted several old friends from the barrel racing circuit and met some of the other visiting queens. Rodeo folks were the most generous in the world, and the girls shared beauty tips and promised to check each other's outfits and makeup before each appearance.

She glanced across the crowded lobby and saw Raeder talking with other cowboys, clearly most of them old friends. She'd never seen him so animated. Lots of backslapping and laughter. She wished she could hear what they were saying. Probably encouraging him about getting back on the bulls.

He lifted RJ into his arms, and the other men made a fuss over him. She was glad Raeder had brought his son. He provided a buffer during their disagreements. And it was fun to show him what went on behind the scenes at the rodeo. Nothing was cuter than the wonder of a child seeing a bigger world.

Raeder watched June as she held Peanut's hand during the line-dance steps. His own feet felt the draw of the lively music, but he didn't dare risk twisting his knee by joining the massive crowd on the conference hall floor. Besides, he was enjoying himself too much watching his son mimic the grownups, giggling when he missed a step. And June's smile showed she was obviously having fun, too. Someday, she'd make a great mom to her own kids.

"That your family?" A chatty older lady Raeder recognized from earlier at the welcome barbecue took a seat across the table from him.

At her question, he drew in a quick breath. To other people they must look like a family, but that was the furthest thing from his mind. "No, ma'am. That's Miss Riverton Stampede—she's a friend of mine, and my son, Peanut. We're up here to promote our rodeo with you folks."

"Well, you sure do look like a family." She watched the dancers for a few seconds. "Did your wife come, too?"

By now, he should be used to this question, but he still

had trouble answering when it came out of left field. "No, ma'am. She's been with Jesus these past four years."

Instead of the usual embarrassment, the gray-haired lady nodded. "Same as my Howard. Sure do miss him. We were married fifty-four years."

Glad to have a way to turn the attention away from himself, he said, "How long's he been gone?"

"Three years. He was a historian and was writing a history of Esperanza. You know Esperanza? It's the little town south of here."

Before Raeder could think of a mannerly question to ask in return, she went on.

"I'm trying to pick up the story from where he left off. The town was founded shortly after the Civil War by a family of ranchers named Northam. They built the Four Stones cattle ranch south of Esperanza. It's still one of the larger ranches in the San Luis Valley. There's a whole series of books about them."

"Northam? Any relation to a Cameron Northam?"

"Why, yes." She blinked her hazel eyes and tilted her head. "Do you know where that boy's gone to?"

Cautioned spiked in Raeder's mind. Surely Cam didn't have a secret life, did he? He was one of June's fellow Sunday school teachers, a deputy sheriff in Riverton, the kind of man anyone who met him knew right away he was good people.

"Um, yes, ma'am, I've met him."

"Well, the next time you see him, tell him folks around here miss him and think he needs to come back. Nobody blames him for what happened five years ago."

The music stopped, and Peanut hopped over to the table. "Daddy, did you see me lime dancing with Miss June?"

Grateful for the interruption before he could get nosy and ask the lady questions about Cam that he shouldn't, Raeder lifted his son onto his lap. "*Lime* dancing? Uh-huh." He forbade himself to laugh. "I did see you out there, Peanut. You done real good, son."

June shook hands with the gray-haired lady, and they commenced talking about rodeo-queen matters. Turned out she'd been Miss Ski Hi Stampede sixty-one years ago.

Raeder thanked the Good Lord for His intervention. The last thing he ever wanted to do was gossip. While he couldn't help but feel a little curious about whatever happened to Cam Northam five years ago, it would have to remain a mystery. Raeder had his own private matters that were nobody else's business.

The next morning, they rose early and prepared for the opening-day festivities. First up was the parade through downtown Monte Vista. As he rode Shadow, with Peanut sitting in front of him, Raeder held one side of the Riverton Stampede banner while June held the other. Folks cheered and waved as they rode past. The float in front of them carried a local high-school drama club in Old West costumes, with the students tossing wrapped candy to the eager onlookers.

"Daddy—" Peanut twisted around to look at Raeder "—can I throw some candy?"

"Sure, buddy. We'll get some for tomorrow's parade. Right, Miss June?"

"Sure. Sounds like fun." She looked her usual pretty self riding on Sprinter in her queen getup.

Her agreement made Peanut happy, and he turned back around to wave at the crowds. And he was by no means the youngest kid riding with a parent. One lady from a well-known local ranching family carried her six-month-old baby girl, all dressed up in Western garb. Raeder called June's attention to his old friend, photographer Bill Jacobs, who stood on a platform shooting the participating marchers.

"Let's give him a wave and a smile. We can use it for publicity."

"Great idea." She put on her gorgeous queen smile, which on her looked genuine, not fake.

"Smile and wave, Peanut." Raeder's own smile felt real, too.

"Have a good ride, Raeder!" someone called out to him from the crowd. Others chorused their agreement.

"Thanks, friends."

They probably remembered him from years past when he competed in their stampede. These were his people, the ones who understood and appreciated all that cowboys went through to entertain them. Maybe he should have signed up to ride in their rodeo this year. Too late for that. But he'd make it up to them next year. He shot a glance at June, who rolled her eyes and shook her head. For some reason, it stung that she wouldn't support him.

Chapter Eight

"Easy, boy. It's almost our turn." June broke her usual rule of not watching her competitors and kept her eyes on the rider now whipping around the barrels.

The girl was good, but a little too frantic and cut too close to the second barrel. Down it went, adding five points to her score. At the end of her ride, the ground crew reset the barrels, and the signal was given. Heart in her throat, June kicked Sprinter into a gallop, racing out of the alley. They spun around the first barrel, dashed across the arena and spun around the second, then moved to the third for a perfect circle, finally making a mad dash back to the alley, barely hearing the wild cheers from the thousands in the bleachers.

"June Mattson and Sprinter, fourteen point two one!"

June released a long breath. The ride had felt much faster, but then, it always did. Maybe she could do better tomorrow.

On the last day, she had her best ride, coming in third overall for the rodeo's four days and earning 838 dollars. Not bad but nowhere near the top purse of 3,756 dollars.

"Don't feel bad." Raeder sat with her at the final party that evening. "You did real good. That Stacy Lockhart has a killer instinct, so she's hard to beat."

"You got that right. Thanks for your encouragement."

June moved RJ's paper plate away from the table's edge so his ketchup-laden fries didn't land in his lap.

"Thanks for saving Peanut's fries. And his jeans."

"No problem." She took a bite of coleslaw. "So after meeting everybody here, we can count our mission accomplished. Everly should be happy with the number of queens and rodeo participants who've put us on their calendars."

"That's what we came for. By the way—" he pulled out his phone "—here's that picture from the parade. I think we look pretty good."

"Wow, that's great. Even RJ's smiling."

"Who's RJ?" The person in question craned his neck to see Raeder's phone.

"Miss June's mistaken." Raeder showed him the picture. "That's you, Peanut." He lifted one eyebrow in a challenge. "Right, Miss June?"

As if sensing the conflict, RJ looked back and forth between her and his dad, his forehead wrinkled with worry. For his sake, she needed to back off. "That's you, all right, sweetheart."

He grinned in his adorable way and went back to eating his fries.

She shouldn't have tried to change his name. No matter how important she thought it was for him not to be called Peanut, she was not his mother and must respect his father's wishes.

The drive south back to Riverton on Monday would take several hours, so they set out early. After checking out at the hotel, they drove to the Ski Hi Complex to hitch up the horse trailer and load the horses. June gladly surrendered the wheel to Raeder. She always felt nervous on these long drives because other drivers often didn't take care in passing her trailer loaded with valuable horses. Leaving Monte Vista behind, they drove to Alamosa and turned south down US Highway 285.

As she had anticipated, on one long straight stretch through Carson National Forest, a tractor-trailer whizzed past them going too fast, causing the pickup and horse trailer to sway toward the edge of the road. June gulped down her nervousness, but Raeder seemed unfazed, his eyes remaining focused on the road ahead as he righted the vehicle's trajectory.

To get past the scare, she tried to enjoy the lush summer greenery bordering the road. Summer winds blew across the highway, causing ponderosa pines and Colorado blue spruce to sway and aspen leaves to flutter. But it was Raeder's steady hands on the steering wheel that truly settled her emotions. She turned to look at him. What was it that made this man tick?

"You looked like you were having a good time with some of your old friends," she told him.

"Yeah, I was. You know how it is. It takes one to know one, and nobody knows us bull riders like, well, another bull rider." His tone held a hit of a challenge. "'Course, they all wanted to know when I'm coming back. I told 'em to come on down to the Riverton Stampede, and they'd find out." He chuckled. "Got a firm handshake from eight of 'em."

Not what she'd hoped for in starting this conversation, but she'd take it as an opening.

"Great. Eight professional bull riders is perfect for that event."

"Nine. Including me."

Not what she wanted to hear. How could she steer him away from it? Maybe another approach. "What about after your bull-riding career does actually end?" She tried to keep the irritation from her voice. "What are your plans?"

"I plan to keep riding until I've made enough money to buy my own place. Until then, between rodeos, I'd like to keep doing what I'm doing at Miss Petra's. And keep on raising my little cowboy." He glanced in the mirror in the direction of his son in the back seat. "Grow some hay. Maybe run a few head of cattle. Set up my repair shop for farm equipment. Give riding lessons to kids. What about you? You gonna compete for Miss Rodeo New Mexico?"

"No. After this year, I want to concentrate on my schooling. Just a few more classes and I'll have my BS. Then I expect to go to vet school in UNM a year from this fall."

"Sounds like a good plan."

She nodded. "Yours, too."

Another tractor-trailer passed them, the wind from its movement rocking the pickup again. Raeder kept them steady. In fact, he was steady in just about everything. She had no doubt he'd do well in whatever he put his hands and mind to.

She glanced back at RJ, who was fast asleep. "Aw, he's so cute. This weekend sure did wear him out."

"Sure did, but he had fun." Raeder chuckled. "Don't know what I'll do to entertain him after the excitement of the rodeo. That is, until the next one."

"Doesn't he have a birthday coming up?" She knew he did. "What are your plans?"

Raeder shrugged. "No firm plans. Maybe take him out for burger and fries. Miss Petra'll probably make a cake."

Ideas swirled in June's mind. "Will you let me throw him a party?" Her excitement grew. "We could invite all the kids from my Sunday school class."

He shot a glance at her, one eyebrow raised. "We?"

For a moment, she didn't know how to answer. Was she overstepping…again? "Well, sure. I'm still his Sunday school teacher for the next seven weeks." Somehow that didn't fully express her love for RJ or her longing to celebrate this special birthday. "I'd like to make him feel special." Still sounded weak.

"Uh-huh." He was quiet for a few minutes, eyes focused on the road. "That's real nice of you. Let me talk to Miss Petra." Another pause. "Just cake and ice cream and maybe a game or two. No need for the kids to bring presents."

"But—"

He shot her a frown and shook his head.

"Well, you should know that all the mothers *will* bring a present."

More quiet. Then, "Yeah, well, I don't really know what mothers want for their child, so…"

As his voice trailed off, June's heart ached for him. She hadn't meant for her simple comment to remind him of his and RJ's tragic loss. Not for the first time she thought how hard it must be for him to raise his son on his own. But he was doing a wonderful job. Her eyes burned as tears tried to form. What could she say to ease his pain for his loss?

"So I'm glad you're here to tell me." He grinned. "As you seem to enjoy doing."

Pulled from her thoughts, she heard only the last part of what he'd said, and her laugh came out on a sob. She coughed it away. She hadn't wounded him after all. "I surely do, cowboy. I mean, we gals are always ready to put in our two cents."

"Ha! With you it's way more than two cents. More like a buck fifty." His face was lit up with a real smile, so she decided not to take offense. He was teasing her. "Okay," he continued, "so presents are fine as long as they're not expensive."

He shot her a knowing look. "At the next kid's birthday party, we won't be able to match anything that costs too much."

"Not to worry. At his age, the fun is in the unwrapping, not how expensive the present is."

"That must be another thing mothers instinctively know." His voice held no sadness, only a hint of humor. "And teachers."

"Right." In truth, she'd love to have a passel of sweet little cowboys like RJ—kids who called her Mom. But that would have to wait until after she finished her schooling. And, of course, it would depend on finding the right man to share life and kids with. Her eyes involuntarily went to the man beside her. No, not him. As attractive and hardworking as he was, she couldn't give her heart to someone who risked his life needlessly for the sake of his sport.

Her phone buzzed and, recognizing the caller ID, she punched the dash to connect to the speaker. "Hey, Everly. What's up?"

"Hey, June. You with Raeder?"

"I'm right here, Ev," Raeder said. "We're driving back from Monte Vista. Got a good report for you. What's happening on your end?"

"Well, we got a little problem with Walt Loggins, our regular NMRA stock contractor. He backed out, so we need you two to work your wonders to persuade him to stick with us."

"Huh." Raeder traded a worried look with June. "Did he say why he's backing out?"

"Said his top-rated stock's too valuable for such a small, two-day venue, and he has too many rodeos to cover this year."

"That's pretty lame," June said. "Don't we have a running contract with him?"

"It was a ten-year contract, and it ran out with last spring's rodeo. When we reached out for a new contract, he hemmed and hawed around and wouldn't give us a decision…until now."

"Sounds like a tactic of some sort," Raeder said. "What's he looking for, Ev?"

"Don't know for sure. Not more money, that's for sure. We already pay top dollar." Everly paused. "You kids up for the job?"

"I'm in." Raeder questioned June with a quick look.

"Me, too."

After they disconnected the call, June looked up Walt Loggins's contact information. "Want to go tomorrow?"

"Sounds good."

She tapped the number in her phone. The call connected right away.

"Loggins Rodeo Stock, Walt Loggins speaking. Caller ID says I'm speaking to Miss Riverton Stampede. That you, June?"

She laughed. "Hey, Walt. How're you doing?" The man was an old friend of Dad's. Maybe that would help persuade him. "Can Raeder and I come over and see you tomorrow afternoon around two?"

"Sure. I'll have Annie fix some cookies and sweet tea."

"Thanks. See you then."

"Good job." Raeder winked at her, then quickly looked away.

Cowboys did a lot of winking at girls, but this was a first for this guy, so it gave her silly heart a little hiccup. She tried to hold good sense up like a shield to her emotions, but the more she hung around Raeder Westfall, the harder it became.

Gripping the exercise bar suspended from a beam in the barn ceiling, Raeder lifted himself off the floor, then counted to a hundred, then lifted his chin over the bar another hundred count. By the time he finished and dropped down to the floor, his arms shook and sweat poured from his face. Earlier this morning, he'd already practiced riding at Cody Martinez's Raintree Restaurant. But no matter how fast or irregular the bucking and twisting of the mechanical bull, nothing could match a real animal. Maybe this afternoon he could talk Walt into letting him lease a couple of his bulls once a week to further his training. And he could take up Cody's offer of more coaching for a minimal fee.

Each day as he exercised, his body remembered more of its former skills, increasing his confidence. With every increase of confidence, he argued inwardly against his father's cutting, demeaning remarks…and June's well-meaning attempts to discourage him from competing in a sport that he loved. To become a champion again meant he must regain his killer drive, the unshakable determination to stay on that bull more than that bull wanted to buck him off. He could do this. He *would* do this. And he'd prove to the scoffers what he was made of. Beyond his own self-respect, he needed to show Peanut how to overcome every adversity life threw his way, whether physical or financial or emotional.

After morning chores and lunch, he and Peanut drove over to June's place, and the three of them headed down to Walt Loggins's ranch several miles outside of Santa Fe. A variety of trees lined the quarter-mile gravel lane leading to the house and a half-dozen other buildings, and cattle and horses fed on the rich green native grass that carpeted the pastures. Massive Brahman bulls grazed in a separate pasture, deceptively passive in appearance.

Raeder caught sight of ol' Spite and Malice, the mean-looking white-and-brown beast that had thrown him bad last year, then stomped on him. *Lord, if it's the last thing I do, let me draw that bull's number and best him.*

"See somebody you know?" June's tone held a teasing note. "An old friend…or enemy?"

"You need to ask?" He'd been knocked out and only later saw the video. It had been brutal, and he could only watch it once. "Did you see it happen?"

"No. I never watch bull riding."

He didn't need to ask why. Seems like she took her brother's crippling injury more personally than Eric, who'd come to terms with the accident that put him in a wheelchair for life. Raeder understood what it meant to take it personally. "I hope you'll keep that under your hat while we're talking to Walt."

She glared at him. "Don't worry. I won't do anything to sabotage our mission. I really do want the stampede to succeed."

"I know." He chuckled. "Just not the bull riding part."

She huffed out a breath. "Just keep driving, cowboy. I see Walt up ahead."

Walt welcomed them to the wide, shady veranda that extended across the front of his one-story redbrick ranch house. His wife, Annie, brought out tea and cookies and set them on the low table in the middle of a group of white wicker rocking chairs. "Y'all have a seat." She waved a hand toward the chairs, then headed back toward the front door. "Walt, you treat them right."

"Yes, dear." He rolled his eyes. "Raeder, it's good to see you up and about. It's been a while. June, you're lookin' as pretty as ever. Now, what can I do for you two?" Looking at June, Walt lounged back, his long legs extended. "Like I don't know. It's just like that old scallywag Everly Strait to send his rodeo queen to win me over."

"Well, then," June said. "How about it? Why not renew your contract with the stampede?"

Walt scratched behind one ear. "It ain't that I don't want to. Over these past ten years, y'all have helped put my rodeo stock on the map. It's just that I've grown and improved my herd, and now, I've bred the best bulls and steers in New Mexico, bar none. I need to not overwork them. Need to save them for the bigger venues like Albuquerque, Clovis and, of course, Santa Fe—venues that last longer than two days. It's a lot of trouble to haul them over to Riverton for such a short event."

Raeder clenched his jaw so he wouldn't say the first thought that came to mind. Didn't this man realize he should be loyal to the folks who'd made him a success? Not something he could say to an older, well-respected person, however.

The screen door opened, and Walt and Annie's tween daughter, Lanie, emerged. She'd grown a few inches since Raeder last saw her, and she gazed at June all starry-eyed. After a few words of greeting, she said, "Miss June, I want to be Miss Riverton Stampede when I'm sixteen. Will you coach me?"

"I'd be proud to, Lanie." She grinned at Walt. "Seems like somebody in this family still likes us."

"Hey." Lanie smiled at Peanut. "Would you like to see my new kittens? They're just two weeks old. Miss June, you can come, too."

Peanut hopped over to Raeder, excitement in his eyes. "Daddy, can I?"

"Sure can. But you be gentle, son." Raeder looked at June. "You make sure he minds."

"I'll do that." June stood and took Peanut's hand. "Let's go."

As soon as they went inside and out of earshot, Raeder

gave voice to his idea. "Listen, Walt, I'm gonna make my bull-riding comeback at the stampede. What would you think of my coming over a couple times a week to practice on your bulls? 'Course I'll pay…and sign a waiver not to hold you accountable if I'm injured."

"Sounds fine to me. You're not the first bull rider to ask me that. We've always got somebody or other out here."

Another idea came to mind, one that had percolated in the back of Raeder's brain for a couple of weeks. "Now, about you providing stock for the rodeo… What would you think of a surprise rematch between me and ol' Spite and Malice? 'Course it couldn't be part of the official competition, 'cause I'll need to draw for my official rides like everybody else. Just an extra added attraction. And it'll publicize how impressive your stock is, which is what you're looking for, right?"

Walt gave him a long look. "You do know that bull's never been ridden for a full eight seconds, don't you? Most anybody's stayed on him is seven point eight." He paused. "Let me think a minute." He scratched his head again. "Yeah. Yeah, I like that idea. We can play it up real big like they do grudge boxing matches." He held out a hand to Raeder. "Let's shake on it, 'cause you got yourself a deal."

Raeder stood and grasped the older man's hand. "We got ourselves a deal."

June returned to the porch to see the two men shaking hands. Did that mean Walt had changed his mind because of Lanie's interest in being Miss Riverton Stampede? Apparently, June needn't have worried about talking to Walt. The Lord had it all worked out.

On the ride back home, Raeder seemed happy, too. They

had much to celebrate, not to mention the good report they could give the stampede committee.

"Daddy, can I have one of Lanie's kittens?" RJ asked from the back seat.

Raeder chuckled. "Son, you got a whole passel of kittens to play with at Miss Petra's place. What are you gonna do with another one?"

"We got barn cats. Lanie's are indoor kittens. I want an indoor kitten." His voice held a hint of stubbornness that sounded much like his father's.

Raeder glanced at June, his handsome face comically creased with befuddlement. "Help me out here?"

She snorted out a laugh. "So *now* you want my help, do you?" She turned around to RJ. "Sweetheart, an indoor kitten takes a lot of work. You need to have a place for their food and water, and have a litterbox you need to clean out every day, maybe more. That's an awful lot of work." She wouldn't mention that her own cat, Muffin, had a kitty door to go outside whenever she needed to. "Besides, you have to ask Miss Petra about that since it's her house. Do you think she wants an indoor cat?"

Disappointment in his eyes, RJ shook his head. "She says cats belong in the barn."

"Well, there you go. Just enjoy those barn kitties for now. Okay?"

"Oookay." The downward tone in his voice on that last syllable signaled surrender.

Raeder caught her eye, gave her his heart-stopping full-face smile and mouthed, *Thank you.*

Added to their success with Walt, that smile made the day seem even brighter. She and Raeder made a good team, almost like Mom and Dad…except they weren't a couple and dear little RJ wasn't her child. Maybe someday she'd have her own family, but that was a dream for the distant future.

Chapter Nine

June credited watching the old *Little Rascals* short films on television for her love of small children. Adorable, smart and witty, those tiny kids had solved crimes, befuddled their teachers and generally caused harmless chaos and mischief. Today, she was reminded of those fictional adventures by the twelve little rascals wreaking havoc on Miss Petra's ranch. Only this time, it was her job to corral them and keep them from harming themselves, the property or any of the animals.

She'd arrived at the ranch early Saturday morning with a bouquet of colorful inflated balloons and a box of inexpensive prizes for the games she and Miss Petra had agreed upon. At RJ's request, they planned to serve hot dogs and potato chips and, of course, ice cream and cake. Miss Petra's large sheet cake was decorated with tiny figures of horses, a barn, a cowboy and even a few chickens. She'd written "Happy Birthday, Peanut" with bright blue icing and topped the cake with five big candles.

The only thing missing before the guests arrived was Raeder.

"Where'd he run off to?" June placed a gallon of Blue Bell vanilla ice cream in the kitchen freezer under RJ's watchful eyes.

"Don't worry. He'll be back soon." Miss Petra bustled about her kitchen, obviously excited about hosting the party.

RJ kept eyeing the plateful of cookies with a hungry look. "Can I have one?" He gave Miss Petra a smile as charming as his dad's. "Please?"

"Now, honey, we don't want to spoil your appetite." Miss Petra set the plate on top of the fridge. "June, can you keep him occupied? Maybe have him help set up the tables and chairs on the lawn?"

"Sure. Let's go, RJ." She reached for his hand, but he gave her a blank stare.

June glanced at Miss Petra, who gave her a puzzled look. "Oops. I mean, Peanut."

"I know what you're doing, honey." Miss Petra shook a finger at June. "But you better be careful there."

"Right." June took RJ's hand and went outside. She'd borrowed plastic tables and chairs from the church, all light enough for RJ to carry. They set them in the newly mowed grassy lawn on the shady side of the house.

By the time they finished tying the last balloon to the picket fence, Raeder drove in and parked his Bronco beside June's pickup.

"Daddy!" RJ ran to greet him, plunging himself into his father's open arms.

"Hey, buddy. You ready to celebrate being five years old?"

June watched their interaction, her heart warming. It would be all too easy to get deeply attached to these guys. Who was she kidding? She already was attached, and it was getting harder to ignore her growing feelings for both RJ and Raeder.

Still holding his son, he ambled over to her. "Say, this sure looks like a party's about to start. Can I come?" he asked RJ.

"Silly Daddy." RJ wriggled out of Raeder's arms.

"Did you feed your chickens?"

"Uh-huh."

"Good man. Now, you stay with Miss June while I go freshen up." Raeder jogged to the back door and disappeared inside.

Where had he been to have worked up such a sweat by midmorning?

The sound of vehicles driving down the lane caught her attention as their guests began to arrive. "Look, Peanut." Hard as it was, she managed to use the accepted name. "Here comes your company."

"Yay!" He clapped his hands and danced around.

Charlotte Sizemore, divorced from a relative of Juliet's father, brought her own two kids plus three others, then took off like a shot before June could ask if she planned to stay and help. Apparently not. The five kids put their gifts on the picnic table Miss Petra had set up for that purpose. Before June could give them any further instructions, they started chasing around the yard and parts beyond.

"Okay, you guys," June called out. "Stick close to the house. Don't be running over to the barn." Too late. The two Sizemore boys had already climbed over the corral fence.

"Hey—" June dashed after them.

An ear-splitting whistle cut through the air, and all the kids froze.

"Get back over here." Raeder's voice held a firm note of authority that brooked no argument. June noticed he'd cleaned up pretty quickly, probably in the house's mudroom, and put on a clean, short-sleeved Western shirt. She tried *not* to notice the impressive bulk of his biceps but failed. Was he working out these days?

The two miscreants climbed out of the corral and slumped back to the lawn. In the meantime, two nosy barn cats had wandered into the party area, no doubt looking for treats. Two of the girls grabbed them while the third pouted. "I want a kitty." She gripped one cat's tail and set it to yowling.

"Stop it!" June barely had time to save the poor creature. She dislodged the child's hand from the tail and sent the kitty running. This was why she taught pre-K Sunday school. Even her child-psych classes didn't give a satisfactory reason for why some kids turned wild at five or six. Even sweet RJ had begun to show a stronger personality.

More vehicles arrived. More kids were dropped off. More moms made their escapes. June began to wonder if this party had been a good idea, but Raeder took it all in stride.

At last, Juliet drove in with her daughter, Sassy, and her brother, Jeff. Juliet set three wrapped presents on the gift table. "We figured you'd need a little help with games and such, so we're going to stick around."

"Miss Juliet, you didn't need to bring presents," Raeder said.

"We wanted to bring presents for Peanut," ten-year-old Sassy said. "Right, Jeffie?"

"Right." Jeff tweaked RJ's nose. "Sure have missed you, Peanut."

"He's missed you, too, Jeff," Raeder said. "By the way, I sure do appreciate you coming over to do chores while I was out of town." He grabbed one of the Sizemore boys by the back of his T-shirt but couldn't quite reach the other one who was untying a helium balloon from the fence.

"Don't do that." June managed to snag its string before it flew away, then surveyed the mayhem. "Oh, my, this sure is a wild bunch. You notice how most of the moms took off. Thanks for staying, Juliet."

"Don't worry." Raeder chuckled dismissively. "We can

handle 'em." At June's doubtful look, he added, "Remember, growing up I had four younger siblings I had to keep in line."

She tucked away that information. One of these days, she planned to ask him more about his growing-up years. He'd hinted at a poor relationship with his father, but clearly he'd had some good influence in his life to make him such a loving and responsible father himself.

"All right, time for games, you guys," she called out. Only RJ paid attention.

Again, Raeder put fingers to his lips and blew out a piercing whistle. "Listen up."

Like so many obedient little soldiers, the twelve children stopped their shenanigans and clustered around, giving the adults their full attention.

"Okay," June said. "First order of business is the three-legged race." That should expend some of their pent-up energy. With gunnysacks borrowed from the church's VBS game stash, June paired the kids with their besties to avoid conflict. As expected, the race brought much falling down and much squealing laughter. The girl who'd pulled the cat's tail pouted over losing. The two boys who won grabbed their prizes—mini Slinky toys—and dashed off to play with them on the back steps.

Next, Raeder and Jeff strung up a makeshift net for a game of balloon volleyball. With several balloons without helium being batted around at the same time and kids jumping around trying to hit them, it didn't matter whether they went over the net or not.

Musical chairs came next. June played music on her cell phone, stopping it after ten or so seconds and watching the kids scramble to sit. Lots of screams, giggles and more falling down ensued as one chair at a time was taken away. With only one chair left for the two remaining kids, June let the music play a little longer. When it stopped, one of June's Sunday school students won the prize, a plastic pen with washable ink.

At last, it was time for lunch. With Jeff's help, Raeder grilled the hot dogs on a charcoal grill, while June, Miss Petra, Juliet and Sassy made sure the little ones didn't come too close. One child dropped her hot dog on the ground and cried her heart out like the world had come to an end. RJ offered her his, which put an immediate stop to the crying. June exchanged a look with Raeder.

"That's so sweet of him."

"Yeah, he's pretty generous." Raeder fixed another dog for his son, who grabbed it and started to dash away. "Hey. What do we say?"

RJ turned back with a grin. "Thank you." He ran to join the other kids seated around the small tables.

Miss Petra brought out the cake, which was a hit with all the kids, each asking for one of the decorating figures. Happily, there were enough to go around. After they sang "Happy Birthday," they all managed to find room for ice cream and cake.

The last game of the day was stick the tail on the donkey." The inexpensive game June had found at the dollar store was a large, shiny poster with a cartoon donkey glancing back to look for its tail. When applied by the blindfolded kids, the colorful sticky tails ended up all over the poster.

Then RJ opened his presents, everything from a Spider-Man T-shirt to coloring books to inexpensive age-appropriate games. Soon the moms started arriving to pick up their kids, leaving the birthday boy tired but happy.

"Somebody's going to sleep well tonight." June began the cleanup, with the others helping.

"Thanks for the party." Raeder touched her shoulder. "He hasn't had this much fun since I don't know when."

His touch sent a pleasant shiver down her arm. "I had fun, too." Her words sounded a little too breathy in her own ears. This cowboy really was getting to her.

Raeder read the story of David and Goliath to Peanut from his kids' Bible storybook, prayed with him, then kissed him good-night.

"Thank you for my party, Daddy." He'd already said it a half-dozen times. Was this a stalling tactic?

"You need to thank Miss June and Miss Petra, too."

"Already did," the boy replied as he stifled a yawn.

"We were all glad to do it, son. Now, you go to sleep so we can wake up and go to Sunday school tomorrow."

Peanut set a hand on Raeder's arm. "Miss June says I won't be in her class after August. Why can't I stay in her class?"

Tired though he was, Raeder settled back on Peanut's bed. "Because now that you're five years old, you get to move up to the kindergarten class. Don't you want to be with the kids your own age?"

"Uh-uh." Peanut shook his head against the pillow. "I want to stay with Miss June."

"I don't—" Raeder started to say "I don't blame you," but that would open a whole other can of worms. "I don't think they'll let you do that."

"Oh." He sighed. "Ooo-kay." His voice dropped lower on that last syllable in his funny way of showing disappointment, and he pulled Ralph the giraffe into a tight hug.

"Okay. So get some sleep…" Raeder tried to stand, but Peanut gripped his arm again.

"Daddy, why does Miss June call me RJ sometimes? Who's RJ?"

Raeder cleared his throat to cover a laugh. "Why, that's you, son." Might as well admit it. "You know your birth name is Raeder James Westfall, Junior. You were named after me. Miss June just happens to think we should call you RJ. But your mama called you her little Peanut, so that's what I call you."

Peanut pondered that for a moment. "Do you think Mama would mind if you called me RJ?"

Raeder swallowed hard. Would Audra mind? With her quirky sense of humor, she'd teased him out of his bitterness over Pa's constant disapproval, saying he'd be the greatest bull rider the world had ever seen. She'd called Raeder her hero, and because of her love, he'd tried to be heroic. She was probably up in heaven laughing at his dilemma about their son's name. *Okay, Audra, how do I get out of this mess you got me into?* Not that he meant to pray to her, just wishing she was here so he could ask her in person.

He looked at his son. "Do you want to be RJ?"

More pondering. "Maybe. Can we try it out?"

Now, Raeder let himself laugh out loud. "Buddy, you can't just keep changing your name. Folks will get confused and won't even know who you are."

"You just called me buddy and son. Miss Petra calls me honey and sugar." He wrinkled his nose. "So who am I?"

Raeder sometimes wondered the same thing about himself. "Those are just nicknames. Folks use nicknames to show they like you."

"Like Peanut."

"Right. Like Peanut."

Another deep sigh was followed by drooping eyelids. Then he blinked, suddenly alert. "I got an idea. Miss June can call me RJ, and you can call me Peanut or buddy or son, like you always do. I don't think Mama would mind."

The earnestness in his five-year-old voice touched something deep inside, and Raeder knew when he was licked. "I don't think so either. You can tell Miss June tomorrow in Sunday school."

Peanut's eyelids drooped again. "Good night, Daddy."

He was asleep before Raeder could bend down and kiss him again. Pretty soon, he'd brush away those kisses, and Raeder would have to find a different way to show his affection. Right now, he felt a surprising satisfaction over their conversation. In making this decision about his own self-identity, his little Peanut had taken another step in growing up. And his daddy couldn't be prouder.

An hour later, as he lay awake in the next room, his mind turned as usual to his upcoming rematch with ol' Spite and Malice. This morning, he'd had a good practice ride on another of Walt's bulls, with Cody giving tips on things he noticed about Raeder's ride. He was regaining his old form and for the most part stayed on these bulls for the full eight seconds. 'Course, Walt only leased him his retired bulls, but the critters still had enough kick in them to prove a challenge each time he mounted them. As he drifted off to sleep, the pictures from Peanut's Bible storybook came to mind. Like David facing Goliath, he would go in the strength of the Lord, conquer the seemingly unconquerable giant and come out victorious. *Lord, I'm working as hard as I can to get ready, but I'm counting on You to make it happen.*

Puzzled, June stared at Raeder, who stood by her classroom door shuffling his feet like a shy teenager, a sheepish grin on his face.

"That's right," Raeder said. "He wants to be called RJ… at least by you."

"You're okay with that?" She couldn't detect anything in Raeder's expression to give her a clue about his true feelings over the change he'd resisted for so long.

Raeder shrugged. "It's his decision."

June squatted down to eye level with the boy. "If you like, I'll be happy to call you RJ from now on."

RJ threw his arms around her neck, almost knocking her off balance. "Thank you, Miss June."

"You're so welcome, P… RJ." She laughed at her own near mistake. She looked toward the door. "Thank you, Raeder. I—"

He'd already left, and other parents were bringing their children into the room, so she stood to greet each parent and child. Though her heart felt warm with this change for RJ, she still felt the usual nostalgia over her students graduating to the kindergarten class. She cared for each one of these precious kids and would miss them. Although her tenure as Miss Riverton Stampede required her to travel to other rodeos on many weekends, she had decided not to miss another Sunday at her home church. And at least her time with RJ—and Raeder—would extend until mid-October as they continued to promote the rodeo.

After the success of one of her suggestions for Raeder's parenting, she would pray for him to see the value of his son learning in a class with other children, whether in public school or in the Christian school that would open in the fall here at the church. If the Lord ever gave her children of her own, she would definitely choose the latter. Now that she considered it, maybe that would prove the one thing that would persuade Raeder to entrust his son to teachers who not only taught essential subjects, but also included the Lord in all of their lessons.

So much for her decision to stop interfering with his childrearing.

Chapter Ten

Raeder wasn't sure it had been a good idea to give riding lessons to the Sizemore boys, ages five and six, but after learning Charlotte Sizemore was a single parent and the boys' pa was in prison, he'd given in. The boys were Jeff's cousins, and he could see they just needed a firm hand when they misbehaved. They also needed a strong male influence in their lives. He'd told their mother she couldn't just drop the boys off at Miss Petra's place and leave, like she had for Peanut's birthday party. She'd have to go for coffee with her friends some other time. For now, she signed the waiver releasing Miss Petra and him from a lawsuit in case of accident.

"Ma'am, you can sit right over there." Raeder pointed to a hay bale right outside the barn door, where she could watch the proceedings. "And I'd appreciate it if you'd keep off your phone during our lessons and pay attention to what we're doing."

"Whatever you say, Raeder." The thirtyish woman fluffed her hair in a flirty way before doing what he'd asked.

"Now, boys." Raeder stood over them, his stance commanding. "When it comes to horses, you can't be running around like you did at Peanut's party." He glanced at Peanut. "Son, you run on back to the big house and help Miss Petra make those cookies."

"But, Daddy—"

"Do what I say, son."

"O-o-o-kay." He shuffled off toward the house, kicking rocks as he crossed the barnyard.

The Sizemore boys watched, eyes wide, probably shocked at Peanut's prompt obedience. Raeder had to stifle a grin. Maybe that would set the tone for their lessons.

"First off, you gotta learn how to take care of your horse." He walked to Darby's empty stall. "Come on over here." He beckoned to them. "See this shovel? This pitchfork?" He nodded at the child-size tools he'd bought for Peanut to learn with. "See that stuff on the floor of the stall? Before you get on my horse, you're gonna clean it out so he doesn't have to walk in it."

Despite their squawking, they finally settled down to work, although it was clear to Raeder he'd have to finish the job later. Next, he took them to the tack room and showed them how to clean the saddle and bridle. "You gotta take care of this stuff so it'll take care of you."

With all the preliminaries tended to, he took the boys outside to the corral. To his surprise, June stood by the fence visiting with Miss Charlotte.

"Hey, June. When did you get here?"

"Just now. I brought your monthly dose of Adequan for Darby, and I wanted to give him a quick checkup." She held out a white bag with her dad's vet practice logo on it. "I hear you're giving Chad and Brody riding lessons."

Raeder took the bag. "Thanks. Yeah, Miss Charlotte thought it was about time they learned about horses." He nodded to the other lady, who looked none too pleased with June being here. "While I give these boys their lesson, would you mind taking this up to the house and putting it in the mudroom fridge?" He handed the bag back to June. "And maybe make sure Peanut's helping Miss Petra make cookies."

"Sure. No problem." After giving him her usual sunny smile, she took the bag back and walked away.

He had a hard time cutting his eyes back to the business at hand.

"Such a nice young girl." Miss Charlotte didn't sound like she believed her own words. "I'd imagine she's got a long line of boys interested in her."

Best to let that drop. "Okay, Chad and Brody, time to meet Darby. You stay here, and I'll fetch him."

He took a lead rope and entered the corral, shutting the gate firmly behind him. Maybe it was Darby's fifteen-hands height—not big for a quarter horse but much bigger than the boys—but they obeyed Raeder, staying outside and peering obediently through the slats in the fence, once again with eyes wide as he led Darby closer.

He'd learned with smaller kids, first his siblings and then his son, that shorter lessons stuck with them better than an overload of information and actions. After fifteen minutes of getting acquainted with the gentle gelding, the two boys had overcome their fears and had gained some respect for both horse and teacher.

"Now, let's see if those cookies are ready."

Miss Petra had advised him that a little reward went a long way to motivating kids, and she was kind enough to provide the perfect treat for his riding students.

June listened to Darby's chest and belly, glad that everything sounded healthy. "He's a good old horse. Dad says he should be around for a long time." She started to put away her stethoscope but paused. "Want me to check out anybody else?"

"It wouldn't hurt to give a listen to Rusty." Raeder tilted his head toward the reddish-gray donkey, who'd come over to the corral fence to find out what was going on.

June did the honors, pronouncing Darby's best friend still healthy and sound as well. She smiled at RJ. "How about you? Should I listen to your heart?"

He giggled. "And my belly."

"Oh, I have a feeling there are too many cookies rumbling around in there for me to get a good reading." She placed the resonator against his chest. "Your heart sounds good."

"Now Daddy." RJ giggled again.

"All-righty." June grinned at Raeder and stepped closer to him, resonator aimed at his chest.

Grinning back at her, he retreated a few steps, waving his hands in front of him. "Oh, no, you don't."

"Da-a-dee," RJ scolded. "It doesn't hurt."

"I don't know about that." Raeder halted his retreat and crossed his beefy arms across his broad chest. "Maybe she'll find out I don't have a heart."

While RJ continued to giggle, June's own heart ached for him. Maybe his heart broke when Audra died. "Well then, we don't want to embarrass your daddy, do we?" She winked at RJ and put away the offending instrument. "My work's done here. Guess I'll see you on Friday when we go down to Clovis?"

Was that a hint of disappointment she saw on Raeder's face? Should she have continued their silly game? Probably not. Besides, she already knew he had a heart, a very big one. From the way he treated the rascally little Sizemore boys to his care for Miss Petra's ranch as if it was his own, he took on both large and small responsibilities other men might ignore, or not even notice. Yes, Raeder Westfall was a man to admire…and she did.

"Yeah. Clovis." Raeder ruffled RJ's hair. "I figure it's a four-hour drive, so we should leave around ten and stop for lunch somewhere near Albuquerque."

"Great. I know a good place to eat on the bypass so we don't have to drive through the city."

Plans made, she packed up and headed home, excited that she would see two of her favorite guys again so soon. When she first had the idea for Raeder to join her in promoting the stampede, she had no idea it would be so much fun or that her whole life…and maybe her heart…would be so involved. The Lord truly worked in mysterious ways.

After a quick drive-through at Chick-fil-A, June drove to Mom's small animal veterinary practice and carried the delicious-smelling lunch inside.

"It's about time." Eric sat in his wheelchair at the front-desk computer, where he was volunteering until Mom could hire a new receptionist. "I'm about to die of starvation."

"Right." June plopped the bag down beside him. "Two grilled-chicken sandwiches, waffle fries, large soda and, because I love you and you need a veggie, kale salad." She pulled out her own order of nuggets, salad and sweet tea. "Eat up, brother."

He grasped her hand. "Lord, thank You for this food and for Your provision and for my bossy little sister. In Jesus' Name, amen."

"Amen." She smirked at her brother. "Your prayer reminds me of how RJ prays. So sweet and innocent and *kind*."

He laughed. "So how is ol' Raeder?"

"Did I mention Raeder? I just mentioned a little boy from my Sunday school class."

"Uh-huh." More laughing between bites. "You have no idea how often the dad's name trips off your lips."

"Oh, you mean when I'm talking about our promotional

trips for the rodeo? Hmm, it would seem mighty strange not to mention the person I'm traveling with."

"Uh-huh," Eric repeated. "By the way, you'll never guess who brought her dog in today. Michelle Walker." He studied one of his sandwiches for a moment, then took a bite.

June nibbled a nugget. How did that woman dare to show her face in this clinic? When it became clear that Eric would never walk again after his accident, she'd left him cold and married one of his fellow bull riders. "And how is she?" June took a long drink of her tea.

"Michelle or the dog?"

She almost snorted the tea out her nose. When she recovered, she said, "Either. Both."

He chuckled, his eyes exuding the peace he'd come to over these past few years. "The dog's expecting. Michelle has a little boy. Her husband died, so she's a single mom." He touched June's hand. "It's okay, sis. Even before my accident, Michelle and I wanted different things…unlike you and a certain cowboy."

She moved her hand away. "Don't be matchmaking for me, Eric. I've got too much schooling ahead of me if I'm to join Mom or Dad in one of their practices."

"Well, the Lord has a way of working those things out."

"Like He did for you?" She gasped. "I'm sorry…" Since middle school, Eric had planned to become a medical doctor, but his injury had ended those dreams.

"It's okay." He took her hand again. "Just please don't be bitter on my account. It'll color all your relationships."

Her brother's words resonated in her mind all afternoon. Was that what she was doing when it came to Raeder?

Most Saturdays in August saw June and Raeder traveling to visit various rodeos within driving distance or June flying to other cities to appear in her role as Miss Riverton Stampede, then hurrying home to teach her Sunday school class. The Riverton committee paid her way in the hope that by supporting the other cities' events, they would reciprocate. All the venues supplied hotel accommodations and horses to ride in the parades and opening ceremonies.

Each time June traveled without Raeder and RJ, she missed their company. Every time she rode with the other rodeo queens, she noticed which ones had the drive to become state and national queens and which ones, like her, were just having a good time representing their local events with no plans to go any further. With eight more months in her reign, she would be making memories to cherish but not dwell on.

The Sunday before Labor Day, she held on to her heart as her six five-year-olds stood at the front of the congregation and graduated to their new kindergarten class. Angie Randall welcomed them in her sweet way, assuring them that they would have a wonderful time learning more about Jesus in her class, as they had in Miss June's. Likewise, June had already met the new four-year-olds who would be with her for the next year. She loved the way her church made a big deal of these promotions so the kids could see how important it was to graduate in their spiritual learning, even more important than in their academic learning.

After the ceremony was over, the kids joined their parents or went to children's church and the service began. Raeder and RJ sat in their usual spot in the second-row pew, where June joined them.

"Want to come out for pizza with my teens?" she whispered.

"Daddy, can we?" RJ said a little too loudly.

"Shh." Raeder tapped his son's nose, as he nodded to June.

The words to the latest popular praise song came up on the screen behind Pastor Tim, and the praise team took their places on the podium. The drummer set the tempo, and the guitars played the intro, while the congregation stood to sing. Joyful music filled the sanctuary, and June added her voice to the worship, as did Raeder. He lifted RJ up on the pew and helped him follow the words. She loved the way he taught his son so many life lessons.

As usual, her thoughts turned to his plans to homeschool RJ. Next Wednesday, classes would begin at the church's new school, and most of them still had room for more students as parents made up their minds between public and private, along with rearranging budgets to make private school possible. But those openings would not remain unfilled for long.

That afternoon, she called the newly hired headmistress of the school. After the usual greetings, she got down to business. "I understand classes will begin this Wednesday. Do you think we could manage a scholarship for Raeder Westfall's son?"

"A scholarship? I didn't even know Raeder was thinking about enrolling his son with us." Glenda Burgess had a master's degree in education and had taught in Riverton's public schools for ten years before moving on to administration for another ten years. She had a vision for creating a school in which the Lord was acknowledged in every part of learning.

"Well, he hasn't exactly said so, but—" How could June explain that she was the one who wanted RJ in school without sounding like she was meddling, even though she was?

"Oh, I understand." Glenda's warm voice held a note of authority. "He can't afford it, and you're guessing if we offer a scholarship, he'll accept."

June paused. That hadn't exactly been her thought, but it sounded good. "I know it would help him if he had options.

He's concerned about RJ being in public school." That was certainly the truth.

"Let me look into it, and I'll get back to you."

"Why not contact Raeder directly?" June held her breath.

"Yes, of course. That would be more appropriate. How thoughtful of you." She was quiet for a few seconds. "June, I'm still filling my lower grade faculty spots, and I have more than enough kindergarten students enrolled to fill a class. I'll probably end up needing a second one. Have you ever considered teaching?"

"N-no, not really. I mean, I love teaching my pre-K Sunday school class, but I've never thought about teaching academics."

"Well, you should. I've heard you're a natural. We could give you a provisional contract while you take some education classes."

Glenda's question hung over June for the rest of the day. All her life, she'd planned to join her parents in one of their vet practices. She loved animals and loved caring for them. But she also loved teaching kids. That was why she was minoring in child psychology. Was Glenda's question the Lord's doing? And how could she figure this out without throwing her parents into a tizzy?

Not fully understanding her own actions, the next morning she found herself driving out to Miss Petra's ranch, where she saw Raeder working on the old tractor in a shed beside the barn. The familiar smells of grease, horse and hay mingled in the air, just like at home.

"Hey, there." He greeted her with his usual grin. "What brings you out this early on a Monday morning?"

She waved away a pesky fly and leaned one elbow against the tractor. "I'm looking for some advice."

He paused and stared at her. "From me? That's new."

She pursed her lips to keep from smiling. "Well, since all my wise counselors are busy today, I'm left with you to ask."

He snorted out a laugh. "Thanks a lot." Grease and oil covering his bare forearms, he reached toward something inside the tractor. "So, what's your problem?"

Did she really want to talk with him about this? Too late to turn back now. "Glenda Burgess asked me to teach in the church's new school."

He stopped working and focused on her, and a comforting feeling spread through her chest. "That'd sure be a switch from vet medicine. How do you feel about it?"

"I'm not sure…"

"Okay, so the first thing you have to do is ask yourself what's your passion. Can you live your life with or without going into vet medicine, or do you feel driven to reach that goal?"

She thought for a moment. Was it a passion or simply what she'd always expected to do, like competing for Miss Riverton Stampede? "I'll have to think about that."

"Okay. So then you need to list the pros and cons of making the change."

She stared at him for a moment. When had he become so wise? "Pros are that I love teaching kids—" she ticked the points off on her fingers "—I'm working toward that minor in child psychology. Glenda says I can have a provisional contract while I take some education classes, which means getting right to work even before I get my degree instead of having four more years of vet school ahead of me."

"Cons?" He picked up a wrench and went back to work.

She dropped her hands to her sides. "I don't want to let my parents down."

Head still bent over the tractor engine, he grunted. "I know the feeling."

This was the opening she'd been looking for these past few months. "Tell me more about your folks."

"I thought we were talking about you."

Stubborn man. "Right. And I'm an open book. My folks have been loving and supportive of whatever Eric and I wanted to do. But like most parents, they do have hopes and dreams for us. It's kinda cute the way they argue over whether I should become a large- or small-animal vet because I know neither one of them will be mad if I choose the other."

"Well, there you have it." He set his wrench in the toolbox and wiped his hands on a well-used rag. "Sounds to me they also aren't going to be mad if you choose something entirely different."

"You're right." This simple truth sent a wave of relief through her, bringing tears to her eyes. "When did you get so wise?"

"Oh, so now I'm wise?" He chuckled, then noticed her tears. "Hey, don't you go crying, 'cause I can't give you a hug with all this grease on me." He blinked and shook his head, like his own words surprised him.

Yes, a comforting hug would feel good right now, but she didn't dare let that happen. Time to throw the attention back on him. "You know, I'm not going to give up asking about your folks."

He frowned and started sorting through his toolbox. After a few moments, he said, "What do you want to know?"

"What happened with your father that made him so distant?" She hoped that was the right word.

He gave her a sideways glance. "Truth be told, I have no idea. Coulda been the war he fought in. Coulda been his own pa. He never talked about his life, and nothing I ever did pleased him. He never believed I could be a success at anything. He scoffed at my passion for bull riding. Never said a thing when I won top prizes. He was the same with my next sister and brother." He shook his head as though trying to shake off a bad memory. "I will say this. Before I left home, he was doing better with my youngest brother and sister. Like he's mellowed or something. I just don't know."

More tears stung June's eyes. She couldn't imagine not having her parents' love and encouragement. "But you didn't follow his example. You're a wonderful dad to RJ."

"I'm glad you think so." He grinned. "Hey, I told you not to cry."

"Sorry. Not sorry." She laughed as she wiped away the bothersome tears. "Speaking of your son, where is he this morning? Have you started homeschooling yet?"

"See, that's what you don't know about homeschooling. School's always in session." He winked at her. "I should have him out here learning about tractors, but he's practicing his printing. Like me, he needs lots of practice with handwriting."

Did he know his winks made her heart skip? Probably not. Unlike most of the cowboys she knew, he seemed unaware of his appeal to women.

His phone sounded with its comical "mooo," and he pulled it from his hip pocket. "Huh. Don't know this number." He started to put it away.

Was that Glenda? June resisted the temptation to try to see the number. "Don't you get curious when somebody you don't know calls?"

He scoffed. "Not really. Probably a telemarketer."

The phone went silent. After a moment, it pinged to announce a voice mail. He shook his head. "They just don't give up." He tapped the phone and put it to his ear. As he listened, his eyes widened. After he disconnected, he looked at June. "That was Glenda Burgess." He frowned. "Did you have anything to do with her offering Peanut a scholarship to the new school?"

As much as she wanted to deny it, she couldn't lie. "Well, I might have inquired…"

He huffed out a harsh breath. "June, I—" He posted his fists at his waist and turned away. "Is that the real reason you came out here today?"

"No. I really needed your advice about teaching."

"Sure you did. Well, you got it, so you can go now." His sharp tone cut into her.

"Miss June!" RJ came running across the barnyard, a paper flapping in his hands. "Look what I did."

She barely had time to gather herself after Raeder's cross dismissal before RJ threw himself into her arms. "What do you have here, sweetie?"

He held out the lined paper. Under his awkward practice lettering he'd drawn a picture. Even as simple as it was, she could still see who it depicted—Raeder, RJ and June, just like a family.

"That's very nice." She managed to choke out the words, then gave him another hug. "I have to go now."

"But Miss Petra wants you to stay for lunch." He gripped her hand.

She looked at Raeder, whose expression had softened. Was it because of his son, or did he regret barking at her?

"That would be so nice, but I have to get back to town." She managed to retrieve her hand without jerking it away. "I'll see you later."

She walked toward her pickup, wishing for all she was worth that Raeder would call her back. But he didn't. And why should she care? In two more months, he would no longer be required to spend time in her company and vice versa. Rather than cheer her, that thought made her even sadder.

Raeder wanted to kick himself. June meant well. He knew that and up to now had been able to deflect her bossy ways. But now, after Miss Glenda's call, maybe he needed to look at this a little deeper. What if June was right about Peanut's education? He'd done real well in Sunday school and at his birthday party. Would he learn better in a classroom with other kids? Raeder had resisted the idea of public school, but if he went to the church's school, there would be a biblical basis for the lessons. With an experienced administrator like Miss Glenda, it would be a quality school, and maybe June could be his kindergarten teacher. He knew Peanut would be happy about that.

He'd seen the hurt in June's eyes. If he didn't have to start mowing hay and working on the chicken coop with Peanut this afternoon, he'd follow her into town and apologize. In the meantime, he needed to call Miss Glenda and discuss that scholarship. If it hadn't been for the ones he'd received and his part-time jobs, he never could have come out of trade school without debt. No matter who offered it, shouldn't Peanut have the same chance? *Lord, this sure is different from what I planned. Give me wisdom as I make this decision for my son. And please, give June wisdom about her future, too. She's a very special person, and I thank You for bringing her into Peanut's and my life.*

Ever since they'd started promoting the rodeo together, he'd felt a growing regret that their partnership would end and he'd have no real excuse for seeking her company again. As mannerly as her wealthy family was to him, he'd never fit in with them. Wouldn't even know how to socialize with them outside of rodeo activities. But he was getting ahead of himself. For now, he might do well to ask her more about the church's school. That was, if she decided to teach there…and, more important, if she forgave him for his rudeness today. Yep, that needed to come first.

He pulled out his phone and punched the autodial for her number. She answered on the second ring.

"Raeder! Is everything okay?"

That was just like her, thinking about somebody else. Any other woman probably wouldn't have answered his call after his rudeness.

"Yeah, everything's fine. Listen, I—" He what? "I'd like to meet you for coffee this evening. Or dessert. You available?"

"Sure. Why not." He could hear the smile in her voice. "What time?"

"Eight. I gotta put Peanut to bed first." Miss Petra had told him more than once she'd babysit if he wanted to go out in the evening.

"Of course. Shall we meet at Mattsons' Steakhouse?"

Now, he was stuck. That was her family's turf. Why hadn't he thought this through?

"Or," she said, "how about Raintree Restaurant? I hear they have flan to die for."

Whew. "Yeah, that works." As long as Cody kept his mouth shut and didn't talk about Raeder's visits to the mechanical bull.

"See you then and there."

It wasn't until Raeder had put Peanut to bed and headed toward town that a worrisome thought popped up. What if June thought he'd asked her for a date? He could tell by her friendly response to his invitation that she wasn't mad at him, so what reason could he give for asking her to meet him? Like the comedian in the old movies, he could only say to himself "this is a fine mess you got yourself in."

Chapter Eleven

June couldn't decide which blouse to wear. Pink or blue or red? Floral pattern or stripes? Should she wear her hair up or down? Raeder hadn't ever said what he liked or didn't like, so she could only guess. She wasn't under any delusion that he meant to ask her for a last-minute date. No, this was simply an apology meeting. He was always quick to apologize for his uncharacteristic rudeness. And she had an apology to give him as well. She really must stop interfering in his parenting. Still, she wanted to look her best when seated across from him at the restaurant.

She decided on the pink blouse, everyday jeans and sneakers, then drove into town and parked next to his Bronco. It was still light outside, but inside, the proverbial party had started. The local country band blasted their music throughout the place, and the aroma of barbecue filled the air. If she hadn't already eaten supper, she'd be tempted to order a rack of ribs and all the trimmings.

As she'd expected, Raeder was waiting inside at the front desk.

"Hey, cowboy."

He grinned in his cute cowboy way. "Hey, yourself."

As the hostess led them to their table, the young woman couldn't keep her eyes off Raeder…and barely acknowledged

June. "I hope we're gonna see you riding the bulls in the stampede next month." She batted her long false eyelashes at him. "I know you'll do real good. You plannin' to ride ol' Cranky tonight?" She tilted her head of over-teased hair toward the mechanical bull some touristy-looking dudes were trying to best without success.

Raeder took off his hat and dropped it on the booth seat. "No, ma'am. Just came for coffee and flan." He looked at June. "That okay with you?"

"Yes to flan. But I'll have herbal tea." June slipped past the hostess and slid into the booth.

"Make that two flans, one coffee, one herbal tea." He sat across from her.

"I'll tell your server." The hostess gave him a too-sweet smile.

She'd barely walked away when an auburn-haired little girl and her mom approached the booth. "Miss Mattson, can I have your autograph?" The child held out a paper napkin and pen. "I want to be Miss Riverton Stampede like you."

"You do?" June glanced at the mother, who looked almost as starstruck as her daughter. "Well, it's lots of fun, but it's also lots of work. Are you willing to work hard?"

"Yes, ma'am." The girl looked up at her mom. "I am, aren't I?"

"You sure are." She squeezed her daughter's shoulder.

June tried to sign the napkin, but it tore. "Uh-oh. Here. I've got something in my purse." She took out one of her business cards with her picture on it and flipped it over to write on the back. "What's your name, honey?"

"Amber."

"What a pretty name for a pretty girl." She wrote "To Amber, future rodeo queen," signed her name, then handed the card to the child. "See you at the rodeo."

"Thank you so much." The mom took her daughter's hand, and they walked away.

"You do that so well," Raeder said. "Did you always want to go for the title?"

"Not really. My family's expected it since I turned sixteen, so I finally agreed to compete last year. Once I got into it, I've enjoyed it."

"Hmm. Sort of like your feelings about being a vet?"

"No." But was it? "Maybe." She sighed. "Until yesterday, when Glenda offered me that teaching job, I would have said definitely no. But that really rattled my cage."

"That little gal sure does want to be Miss Riverton Stampede, like it's a passion. I've asked you what's your passion. Have you figured it out yet?"

"Nope." She laughed. "I've planned to follow my parents' path for so long I don't even know what I want. It's part of me."

Their server, one of June's teens from church, brought their order. "Hey, Miss June, Mr. Raeder." The perky brunette set the drinks and dessert in front of them. "Can I get you anything else?"

"That'll do it. Thanks." Raeder reached across the table to June. "Let's pray."

June slipped her hand in his, noticing the dark stains from his work on the tractor deeply ingrained into his skin. The warm touch of his hard-won callouses sent a pleasant sensation up her arm. Oh, my. This guy was really getting to her.

"Lord, we thank You for this special treat and for the folks who prepared it. Use it to strengthen our bodies and our hands for Your service. In Jesus's name, amen."

"Amen." June forced herself to release him before he got the wrong idea. She took a bite of the caramel-covered custard. "Mmm. So delicious."

"June, I'm sorry for being rude to you this morning." His eyes on her, Raeder held his spoon suspended over his dessert. "I know you want the best for Peanut. I've been raising him alone for a long time, so it's not easy to let somebody come up with other ideas. Will you forgive me?"

She sipped her tea. She wanted to say "no problem," but that would sound like she was brushing off his apology. "Yes, of course. And I understand. Well, sort of. I'm not a parent, but I've babysat my younger cousins growing up. And, of course, teaching my little pre-K kids." She laughed softly. "Guess that makes me an expert…or makes me think I'm one." At his grin, she continued. "Will you please forgive me for trying to interfere with the wonderful job you're doing as a dad?"

"Sure will." He finally took a bite. "Yeah, this is pretty good." After a second bite, he said, "Turns out your so-called interference isn't so wrong after all. I talked with Miss Glenda this afternoon, and we're gonna give her school a try. Peanut was real excited about the idea."

June had to swallow hard to keep her emotions in check.

Raeder took another bite. "'Course, it'd be real good if you were his teacher, but I'm not gonna pressure you to change the direction of your lifelong plans on such short notice just for my son." He settled down and devoured the rest of his flan, washing it down with his coffee. "You gonna finish that?" He pointed his fork at her half-eaten dessert.

"Uh, yeah, I am." She lifted her arm protectively over her plate. "You want more, you can order it."

Chuckling, he raised both hands in surrender.

"Hey, Raeder." Cody Martinez approached the table. "Couple of guys over there—" he hooked a thumb over his shoulder "—want to challenge you to a ride on ol' Cranky."

Raeder didn't look where Cody pointed to but muttered, "Thought we had an agreement."

Cody shot a look at June. "Sorry. This didn't come from me. They recognized you and wanted me to ask." He shrugged. "Gotta keep all my customers happy."

Raeder blew out a long breath. "Tell 'em no thanks. They'll see me— Never mind. Just say no thanks."

"You got it." Cody walked away, then came back. "Your order's on me."

"That's not necessary."

But Cody had already walked away again.

June bit her lower lip to keep from asking the obvious and *interfering* question. What was Raeder's agreement with the restaurant owner? Cody used to ride bulls in the rodeo. Was he encouraging Raeder to return to the arena? Just when she'd begun to think their friendship could go deeper, she was reminded of his foolish determination to risk his life for the sake of proving…what? To prove his worth to a faraway father who couldn't care less?

They'd made up after this morning's unpleasantness. She couldn't—wouldn't—risk another argument. But she would continue to pray that, for the sake of his son, this dear man would get some sense in his thick head.

Raeder owed Cody an apology. Of course, he'd kept his word. And that hostess didn't know anything. She was only being friendly. And Cody just wanted to make his other patrons happy. But Raeder didn't want people watching him practice, as some fans liked to do. Things had gone pretty well out at Walt's ranch, with Cody's knowledgeable coaching fixing the bad habits Raeder had fallen into once he started riding again.

He dismissed his ruminations and focused on the sweet lady across the table. "You don't look happy. What's going on?"

June shook her head. "It's nothing."

He'd been around her long enough to know that wasn't true, so he gave her a minute.

"Raeder, I—" She shook her head again. "No use going over old territory. You know I'm praying you won't ride again."

"I do know that." Still, it stung that she said it. "But it's something I have to do. You know that passion I was talking about? That's what I feel about bull riding. Ever since I was sixteen, I've worked hard to become a champion. I'm not going to let one bad ride defeat me."

Her eyes got red, and she looked down at her empty plate. Maybe it was because she didn't have a passion of her own that she couldn't understand his. It wasn't fair to compare her to Audra, but he couldn't help himself. His wife had been his biggest cheerleader and encourager. She made him promise to keep riding for Peanut's sake after she was gone. As much as he liked June—cared for her, actually—he couldn't see going further in their friendship if she couldn't support him in the one thing he needed to do to restore his belief in himself. And, of course, prove to Pa that he could conquer hard things. *And* to set an example for his son.

"I do admire your resolve." She gave him a sad smile. "Just not your application."

He chuckled. "So…agree to disagree?"

"I suppose." She bit her lower lip. "Raeder, it's not that I doubt you have the drive to get back on a bull. I'm sure you do. So did Eric. And look where that got him. 'One last ride,' he promised Mom and Dad and me. And that's all it took to ruin his life. It's not like he needed the prize money, like so many bull riders do. And for what it's worth, I'm not sure he even had that passion you're talking about."

He let her words hang in the air for a few minutes. Maybe she didn't know her brother as well as she thought. Eric did feel a passion for bull riding or he wouldn't keep up with others still in the sport. And he might not have needed the prize money, but Raeder sure did if he was ever going to have his own ranch or be able to raise Peanut without scraping by. Coming from money, June would never be able to understand, so he let it be. One more reason not to let go of his heart, which stubbornly kept pulling him in her direction.

They'd come here tonight to trade apologies, and they'd done that. Now, they were leaving with a shadow still clouding their friendship. But what could he do? After the rodeo, he wouldn't have to see her anymore…unless she took that teaching job and Peanut ended up in her class. Which he hoped would happen. Which only proved his foolish self-contradiction with regard to this woman.

By the time they left the restaurant, it was dark outside. He walked her to her truck, then followed her home, waving goodbye once she was safely on her front porch. Tomorrow, he and Cody would drive down to Walt's for more riding practice on the bulls Walt set aside for the purpose. Every time he laid eyes on ol' Spite and Malice, his determination grew. He would ride that unrideable critter for a full eight seconds, no matter what it took.

Early Wednesday morning, June stood with Glenda in her own pre-K Sunday school room that would serve the overflow kindergarten class. She surveyed the room, eager to work with her students for however long she was with them. She'd already told Glenda she'd take the position only until they could find an accredited teacher. And Glenda would need a sub on some Fridays while June fulfilled her rodeo duties.

When June had surrendered to Glenda's gentle coercion and taken this job, she'd expected to feel trapped. She always found it hard to say no when people asked her to help out, whatever the project. This time she felt excited. Four of the six kids who'd graduated out of her Sunday school class would now be in this one, including RJ, and she was pleased to see they would again be in her care. The class was to be capped at sixteen, seven more than her Sunday school class, and there were already thirteen on her roster. She looked forward to meeting both old and new students in another half hour. Chad Sizemore's name was on the list, which gave her a moment of concern. Good thing she'd asked Glenda what the school's discipline policies were.

Glenda put a hand on her shoulder. "You're going to do great. I just know it. Do you have any questions on the curriculum I gave you?"

"No. I've already organized my lesson plans. I think I'm ready." A study of the materials had revealed she would teach reading, phonics, basic arithmetic, art and simple science, the latter of which would put to use her university science classes. She'd also be helping the kids learn to share and play nice together.

At eight o'clock sharp, she followed Glenda to the church's fellowship hall, where students, parents and teachers had assembled. Pastor Tim welcomed everyone and prayed for a blessed, Jesus-filled school year. Glenda made opening remarks, then introduced the teachers. Each teacher called her or his list of students, who, along with their parents, were to follow them to the Sunday school building. June led her group to her classroom and stood at the door as they filed in.

"Parents, please line up along the front—" she indicated

the wall with its shiny new whiteboard "—and kids, you can find a seat around one of the tables." It was best to let them choose so they could sit next to a friend or, in the case of the identical Ortman twins, a sibling. It would be tricky to tell those little girls apart.

She hadn't seen Raeder since Monday night, and she felt a little hiccup near her heart when he gave her his winsome smile as he passed by, hat in one hand and holding on to RJ with the other. Or maybe her emotions were stirred by RJ's confident walk to his usual seat and the friendly way he played host to some of the other students, helping them find a place to sit. In addition to showing leadership qualities, this precious little boy sure did copy his father's gentlemanly ways.

After the last parent and child entered, June closed the door and walked to the front of the room. "Welcome, children, parents. I'm so glad to see you all. I'm Miss Mattson." She then asked the parents to introduce themselves and their child. "Very good. Parents, today, we'll be in class for a half day, so you can pick your child up at noon. Starting tomorrow, please provide your child with a bag lunch and a mat for naptime, as we'll be in class all day. Before you go, do you have any questions?"

After answering several queries, she dismissed the adults. One little girl seated beside RJ cried out for her mommy. The woman stopped at the door, casting a doubtful look at June.

"Don't be scared." RJ set a hand on the girl's shoulder. "Miss June, I mean, Miss Mattson's real nice. You'll see."

The girl looked doubtful but settled back in her chair.

"She'll be fine," June said to the mom, who quickly left.

"You're doing great," Raeder whispered in her ear as he passed her, then disappeared into the hallway, leaving behind the mild fragrance of his Stetson aftershave.

She shook off the pleasant shiver his whisper and scent had caused, and returned to the business at hand. By the time the first parent returned at noon, June had memorized each new child's name, assessed their reading and arithmetic skills, taught them two songs about Jesus and let them color the pictures Glenda had provided. She'd also decided this was the most fun she'd had in ages. Every one of her thirteen students was a delight, even Chad Sizemore…without his older brother to lead him into mischief. Like her pre-K Sunday school kids, this bunch came up with the funniest questions and ideas. She already loved them and could see herself teaching full-time. Was this the passion Raeder had talked about?

Now, to figure out how to manage the rest of her obligations. She and Raeder needed to stay on top of the rodeo arrangements, she needed to practice her barrel racing and she needed to take evening classes to finish her degree, including adding those education classes to her academic schedule. And, of course, she needed to finish her queen year, which meant continuing to visit other rodeos or rodeo committees to keep up their interest in the Riverton Stampede.

It was a lot to accomplish. But she trusted the Lord would sort it out for her, as He always did.

With the tractor fixed and the hay mowed, Raeder felt at loose ends. He'd planned to spend his mornings teaching Peanut his lessons but with him in school, that responsibility now rested with June. The place felt empty without his little sidekick hustling along beside him wherever he went. Maybe Miss Petra had some odd repair jobs around the house for him to do.

He found her in the kitchen making her daily batch of

bread and cookies. "My, oh, my, Miss Petra, this place always smells so good."

"I'm glad you like it. Bread's ready to slice, so sit yourself down." She took the tea towel off a fat loaf of warm sourdough bread and took her favorite serrated knife from the wooden knife block. "Got a question for you, Raeder."

"Yes, ma'am." He took the slice she handed him on a plate and buttered it from the crock on the table.

"You think you can run this place by yourself?" She was busy with slicing more of the loaf so she wasn't looking his way, otherwise she'd have seen his jaw drop down to his knees.

"You goin' someplace?"

"Aw, I can't decide." She blew out a big sigh. "That Zeke Baldwin makes me so mad."

Raeder swallowed a chuckle. Poor ol' Zeke had been trying to court Miss Petra from way before Raeder moved to the ranch. She'd rejected the old cowboy, saying until he came to Jesus, he'd just as well forget about her. Now that he'd come to Jesus *and* joined the church, she could no longer claim that excuse. "What's he done now?"

"Well, he's up and proposed to me." She shot a quick glance at Raeder.

"You don't say." He managed an expression of polite interest.

"That's the trouble." She scowled. "I do say." She set her knife down and wrapped the bread slices in the tea towel, then shot him a look over her shoulder. "What'm I gonna do, Raeder? I've lived on this here ranch all my life. It's been in my family since 1880. Even lived here with my scoundrel husband 'til he up and left me for Jeff's mama, Brenda." She stared out the window for a moment. "How'm I supposed to get married and move away at my age?"

She was maybe fifty-five, sixty at the most, Raeder figured. Not exactly ancient.

"Well, ma'am, I guess an even more important question is are you better off with him or without him? Zeke, I mean. Not Dillard." Actually, the question worked for both men. Her ex had murdered poor Brenda last Christmas and was in prison awaiting trial. She was definitely better off without him.

Hands on hips, she turned to face him full on. "Now, why do you have to go and ask me that?"

He'd never heard her so grumpy, never seen her mad at him, and it made him laugh. "Back to your original question. Do I think I can run this place by myself? Sure can. Feel free to marry Zeke, knowing your land is in good hands." He thought for a moment, his heart sinking to his stomach. But he owed it to her to ask. "Why not have Zeke move over here?" Which, of course, would mean he and Peanut would be out of a home, and maybe him out of a job.

"Boy, have you ever seen Zeke's house?"

"No, ma'am." From the way the old cowboy dressed— clean but rumpled—he looked like he wasn't much concerned about appearances.

"It's brand-new. He built it himself. Everything's shiny and up-to-date. Appliances and everything." She looked like she was about to cry. "Said he built it for me."

At that revelation, Raeder felt a bit emotional himself. "Wow. That's impressive. Shows he must love you a whole heap." What would he do for the woman he loved…if he loved one? June's beautiful face came to mind, but he shut that down quickly. "I know you need to think about it 'cause you can't make such a big decision like marriage based on what he gives you or does for you or even if he loves you. The question you have to decide is do you love *him* and want to spend the rest of your life with him?"

She got a wily look on her face. "How 'bout you ask yourself that same question 'bout a certain young lady you been spending so much time with lately."

He glanced up at the old clock above the old refrigerator. Both had probably been there since her grandparents ran the place. "Speaking of time, got a boy to pick up from school." As he hurried out of the house to his Bronco, he could hear Miss Petra laughing like he'd said something funny. *Whatever.*

He drove to the church, eager to see how Peanut's first day had gone. Along with other parents, he pulled into the line in the parking lot in front of the Sunday school building. He was glad to see Deputy Cameron Northam standing watch as the school resource officer. He'd never delivered that message from the lady in Monte Vista, so with a few minutes until noon, he parked and approached the lawman.

At six foot two, maybe six-three, Cam no doubt intimidated most lawbreakers. To his friends like Raeder, his friendliness and Christian character were the qualities to admire. After greetings, handshaking and shooting the breeze for a bit, Raeder considered how to bring up the subject.

"When we were up at the Ski Hi Stampede, your name got mentioned by a lady June and I were talking with."

Cam's friendly expression clouded, and he turned a shoulder toward Raeder, staring out across the line of parent cars. "That so?"

Raeder swallowed. Should he continue? Whatever happened in Monte Vista wasn't any of his business, yet the lady's message might encourage this good man.

"She wanted you to know that nobody blames you for what happened five years ago. And everybody hopes you'll come back some day."

The newly installed school bell rang, and Raeder could

hear a commotion inside the building. Shortly, older students began to exit, while parents of younger kids waited by the classroom door for their teachers to bring them out. Amid the disorder, with Cam directing both foot and vehicle traffic, he caught Raeder's eye and gave him a nod, the kind that said "thank you." With a boy to fetch, Raeder couldn't ruminate on the other man's life, so he swam upstream in the river of students and made his way to June's classroom.

As June did with her Sunday school class, the kids were lined up at the door for parents to claim them. Each child held papers with colorful artwork and practice writing, including Peanut.

"'Bye, RJ." A little blond girl gave him a cute smile.

"'Bye, RJ," said several other kids.

With his son not correcting them but returning his own goodbyes, Raeder had the feeling he'd lost a battle about his son's name. It didn't bother him as much as he thought it would, but it would be a long time before he'd quit calling his little boy Peanut.

Peanut brought him his papers and took his hand. "I'm hungry, Daddy. Can we get a burger?"

"Let me think about that."

Raeder watched June's interaction with the other parents as they left the room. She walked to her desk looking as fresh as she had earlier that morning. Or so it seemed to him. Today, she didn't wear fancy queen makeup like she did for their rodeo promotion trips, and her long blond hair was pulled back in a low ponytail. She looked like an outdoor girl, just as she had the day of their picnic several months ago, one of his favorite memories of his times with her that soon would end. He would miss those outings for the rodeo.

After the last parent and child left, he spoke without thinking. "Hey, June. Want to get a burger with Peanut and me?"

"Oh." She looked up from sorting papers on her teacher desk and smiled. "Hey, Raeder. Yeah, that sounds great. Let me get my stuff together. These kids are going to challenge me, and I need to be prepared." She stuffed papers and books into a satchel.

And just like that, as though they had an understanding, they wound up in his Bronco in the drive-through parking lot, chatting about their morning like it was the most natural thing to do. How long could this go on? How long before some rancher or doctor or businessman came along to capture her heart, somebody worthy of a beautiful, well-heeled lady like June Mattson, and Raeder wouldn't be able to enjoy these times with her anymore? But as he listened to her talk about each of her students with such enthusiasm, his own concerns faded, and all he wanted was to be her good friend and listening ear.

"You wouldn't believe the difference in Chad Sizemore," she said. "Without Brody in the same class, he's surprisingly well-behaved. And I'm already figuring out how to tell which Ortman twin is which. April is quiet and studious, and May is talkative and outgoing, always the first one to have her hand up to answer questions."

Raeder chuckled. "Do you realize you haven't stopped talking about your kids since you got in the car?"

"Really?" She blinked those pretty blue eyes. "I'm sorry—"

"No, it's all good." He dipped a Tater Tot in ketchup and popped it in his mouth. "You had a much more interesting morning than I did... Mowing hay, feeding the cattle, everyday stuff."

They ate quietly for a few minutes. Even Peanut didn't pipe up as he usually did.

June finished her burger, wadded up the wrapper and put it in the take-out bag. "Y'know what?"

He laughed. "What?"

"I really like teaching. I know this is just my first day. Well, not counting Sunday school. But it's amazing how open these little minds are, and eager to learn. What a blessing to be the one who gets to pour in knowledge and faith." Her brow furrowed like she was considering her next thought. "It's not that I don't love taking care of animals, but—" She scowled at him. "You know this is all your fault."

He laughed again. "Sure. Blame the nearest cowboy. Why's it my fault?"

"If you hadn't talked about having a passion for my goals, I don't think I would have accepted Glenda's offer so I could see if this was a better fit for me than being a vet." She sighed. "What am I going to do? What am I going to tell my parents?"

She wasn't really asking him, but he'd answer her, anyway. "Look at it this way. If you still feel this way by the time you get your degree, you can teach during the school year and work as your dad's or mom's vet assistant in the summers."

She turned those blue eyes on him again, and his heart did a backflip. He really had to stop reacting to her beauty. "So, Mr. Westfall, exactly when did you get so wise?"

He scoffed. "Yeah, you accused me of that a while back. But remember, I helped raise my four younger siblings."

Thoughts of those four siblings stuck with him the rest of the day, and as he lay in bed that night trying to sleep. He knew he should have kept in touch with them after Audra died and he went out on the rodeo circuit with Peanut in tow. Should have let them know about his accident. His sister Ally would have his head for not telling her, at least. They'd been closest in his growing-up years, and she'd been real mad when he didn't invite her to his wedding. But he'd figured his siblings were still too scared of Pa to cross him, even though Ma had. And he had to credit Ally and Giselle for sticking by him when Audra was sick. After Audra died, and Ally offered to take Peanut in so Raeder could continue his bull riding, he'd told her that as long as he was alive, he wasn't about to let anybody else raise his son.

Water under the bridge, as the saying went. Yet suddenly he had an itch, a yearning to find out how they all were getting along. June had called him wise. He didn't think so, but if it was true, maybe it was time to put that wisdom to use in his own life…if he could figure out what that was.

Chapter Twelve

"Used to be a man could count on folks to keep their word."
Holding a paper in his hand, Everly Strait scanned the faces
of committee members seated around the table in the arena
conference room. "We got two weeks 'til the stampede, and
three serious problems to solve. Gregg Banners is closing
their doors and have canceled all orders, including the ones
we were counting on. We can use last spring's stampede banner and just paste October over May. But our sponsors ain't
gonna like not having shiny new banners to post around the
arena during the rodeo. Every local banner maker I've called
on says they're too booked up to do so many of 'em for us in
time for our event. You'd think they'd want to support their
own community events."

June leaned across Raeder and whispered to her cousin.
"Rob, are you still friends with the owner of that banner
place in Santa Fe?"

"I was thinking about them, but let me look into it before
I say anything."

"Our next problem," Everly said, "is George Alslip's de-
veloped a nodule on his vocal cords, needs surgery, so he's
had to bow out of announcing for us. I don't have to tell you
that the announcer can make or break a rodeo."

Groans sounded around the table.

Cousin Rob had done some announcing in his younger years. Nobody knew rodeo like he did, all the details that informed and excited the crowd while they watched the various events. June gave him another look. He responded with a sharp shake of his head. She'd have to work on him. Or ask his new bride, Lauren, to do it for her. Or maybe the four kids in their blended family.

"Last, but by no means least, our local band that's supposed to play for our kickoff supper and dances the next two nights got a call from a Nashville recording company to come now or never, so they won't be with us. Good for them. Not so good for us."

"We could find a DJ," Zeke said.

"Ugh," Miss Petra said. "Canned music. Nobody wants that."

June looked at Raeder. "Any ideas?"

"Nope." His brow furrowed like he was thinking hard, then he shook his head. "Sorry."

June raised her hand. "Everly, we'll come up with something." Maybe the high-school bluegrass group would rise to the challenge.

"Thank you, June. Now, that was the bad news. The good news is that Webberley's Carnival is due to set up three days before the rodeo. We got fifteen food trucks lined up with plenty of variety. And according to Nancy—" he nodded to Nancy Snow at the other end of the table "—everything for the Riverton Fair and 4-H Show is getting set up as we speak. If nothing else, we'll pull everything together for all those kids who've been working so hard on their projects."

Raeder was the first to know. Right after he finished the milking and a little while before Peanut usually came downstairs for breakfast, Miss Petra quietly announced to him that she'd finally given up the fight. She and Zeke would be going to the courthouse today to tie the knot…and would Raeder stand up with them?

"Yes, ma'am!" True joy for his boss lady flooded him. Whatever they decided about this ranch didn't matter. These two were the most generous folks he knew in a community of generous people. They deserved happiness. The Lord would provide for him and Peanut, as He'd always done. "What time? I'm available as soon as I take Peanut to school at eight."

"We're meeting the preacher at nine. No use putting it off any longer." From her tone, one would think she was headed for the gallows, but the twinkle in her eye told a different story. "He won't quit pestering me, so I told him I'd marry him just to make him stop."

Raeder decided to play along. "Well, what can you do with a man like that? Might as well surrender. So what do you want me to do? Give you away or be best man?"

She stared out the kitchen window. "Everly's gonna stand up with Zeke. Guess it'd be too much to ask you to be my bridesmaid."

Raeder almost spewed his coffee. Once he regained control, he said, "Sure. I can do that. Long as I don't have to wear a dress."

"Oh, well, then. Hmm." She studied him. "Raeder, you're like a son to me so I guess you'll have to give me away." Her voice broke a little, betraying her true feelings. "Guess I'll have to call on Juliet to do the honors of being my matron of honor."

Raeder regarded her for a bit. "If you don't mind me asking, how come you aren't getting married at the church? Having everybody come and celebrate with you?"

"I don't want people making a fuss."

"But two good people getting married is worth a big fuss." His words circled back to bite him. He and Audra had married at the preacher's house with little to no fanfare. He'd always planned to give her a second wedding, the one she deserved once he could afford it. Then Peanut came along. Then cancer. Then she was gone.

"Aw, don't harp on it, Raeder. We got the stampede and county fair to deal with in less than two weeks. Besides, Zeke don't want folks fussing over us, either."

"I want to fuss over you, Miss Petra." Peanut came bouncing into the kitchen, ready for school except for the misaligned buttons on his school uniform shirt. He threw his arms around her waist.

"Aw, sweetheart." She bent down to kiss his forehead, then fixed his buttons. "Now, you sit down and eat your breakfast. I got your lunch fixed and ready to go."

"Thank you, Miss Petra." He climbed into the booster chair he wouldn't need much longer.

Raeder's heart hitched. What would their mornings be like after his boss lady got married? What would their lives be like?

Taking Peanut to his classroom, he had to bite his tongue not to tell June about the wedding. Good thing she was busy greeting her students, so he wasn't tempted above what he was able to resist. Instead, he waved to her as Peanut ran into the room, glad to be with his friends and his beloved teacher.

At the courthouse, he found all the participants except Zeke. As the minutes ticked past nine o'clock, Miss Petra, decked out in her prettiest Sunday dress, looked like she was trying to be mad, but Raeder knew her well enough to see her vulnerability. His respect for the groom was beginning to crumble right up until the door to the courtroom burst open and two deputies hauled him in.

"I'm here! I'm here!" Zeke hustled toward the front of the judge's bench where Pastor Tim waited to officiate.

"Where you been, you old scallywag?" Miss Petra didn't sound as much angry as she did relieved.

"I'm sorry, darlin'." Zeke kissed her cheek. "I had a flat tire, and these two fine young deputies stopped to help me out. When I told 'em I was late to my wedding, they drove me here with sirens blazing." He shook hands with the two men. "Thanks, fellas. Stick around and you can have some cake."

"Thanks, Mr. Baldwin," the older deputy said. "But we've got to get back to work."

"Congratulations," the other said as they walked out.

"Flat tire, eh?" Miss Petra seemed about to launch into a scold.

"Dearly beloved—" Pastor Tim almost shouted the words. "—we are gathered here together to unite these two in holy matrimony. Miss Petra, you still want to proceed?"

"Oh, I suppose."

By this time, Raeder, Juliet, Everly and the court clerk didn't even try to stop laughing. Somehow, the rest of the wedding happened. Pastor Tim completed the ceremony when he said, "I now pronounce you husband and wife. Zeke, you may kiss your bride."

Face bright red beneath his weathered tan, Zeke did as instructed, then faced the others. "Y'all come on over to my—" He looked at Miss Petra with tender affection. "To *our* house for some refreshments."

Raeder was happy to join the celebration. The weather was good, Darby and Rusty were out in the pasture and the hay could be baled this afternoon, so he followed the new-lyweds out to Zeke's home on the far side of Riverton from Miss Petra's. As promised, a tasty-looking three-tiered wedding cake sat in the middle of the brand-new mahogany dining room table, along with bowls of nuts and mints on one side and triangle jalapeño pimento cheese sandwiches on the other. And, of course, coffee. After everybody ate their fill, Pastor Tim and Everly said their goodbyes, and Raeder started to do the same.

"Hang on a minute." Zeke beckoned to him. "Have a sit." He indicated a plush new chair in the living room. "Juliet, you sit, too."

"Come on, Raeder." Miss Petra's daughter smiled at him. "No sense arguing with my new stepdad."

"Wouldn't want to, anyway." He took his seat across from the couple. He owed a lot to Miss Petra for taking him and Peanut in after his accident, so he'd be fine with whatever they asked him to do.

"My wife—" Zeke said the words with a catch in his voice, so he cleared his throat. "My wife and I came to a decision the other day. Well, she wasn't my wife yet, but you get my drift. Anyway, Juliet's agreed to it, too. With her being Miss Petra's heir, we thought it only right to get her okay on this."

Raeder's chest tightened. What did this have to do with him?

"Quit yapping and get down to business." Miss Petra swatted Zeke's arm. "Oh, never mind. Raeder, I want to sell you my ranch."

Raeder hadn't been this stunned since ol' Spite and Malice stomped on him a year ago. "I—I…" He turned to Juliet. "You're okay with this?"

She smiled. "Sure am. And Sam agrees. Sassy and Jeff and I are very much at home living on the Double Bar M Ranch. With Mama living here in this beautiful new home Zeke built for her, I can't think of anybody else I'd like to see owning and running Murphy Ranch."

Raeder couldn't even find thoughts, much less words to answer with. His own place? It was a dream come true. But how would he pay for it?

"We're thinking you might consider turning it into a dairy farm." Zeke must have read his thoughts. "With Maude and Chloe being such fine milk producers, you could add a few more cows—"

"Stop that, Zeke." Miss Petra rolled her eyes. "Let the boy make his own mind up about how he wants to run the place." She looked at Raeder. "That is, if you want to accept our offer."

His eyes burning, Raeder swallowed hard and gritted his teeth, forbidding himself to let the tears form. *Lord, if this is from You, I know You'll work out the details.* "I'd be pleased and proud to accept your offer. I'll work hard to pay—"

"Of course, you will."

"We know you will."

Miss Petra and Zeke spoke at the same time, then shared a look and laughed. Zeke added a kiss to his wife's cheek, and she leaned into his shoulder for a moment.

"All right." Miss Petra stood. "You two can go now. I got dishes to wash and furniture to rearrange. Zeke, pack up some of that cake for Peanut and for Sam and Juliet's kids."

"Yes, dear."

Every time Raeder was about to sit on a bull, he said a prayer and centered his thoughts and emotions on the business at hand. Now, driving across town back to the ranch, he went through the same routine to avoid causing a wreck. Except now, he was shaking like aspen leaves in the wind at this possible change in his life. His own ranch. A place to fix up just the way he wanted. A home to raise Peanut and provide him with a legacy. Something he'd thought would take him years to achieve.

As he drove past the church, the urge to stop and give his good news to Peanut, and June, of course, almost overwhelmed him. But a parent couldn't just barge into a classroom like that. It would have to wait. Then another thought stunned him, and he had to slow down. Owning his own land meant he would no longer be a poor cowboy with nothing to offer a woman. Sure, the Murphy Ranch couldn't hold a candle to the vast Double Bar M Ranch, or even the much smaller place June's parents owned. But he could build it up, make something of it. Maybe a dairy farm, as Zeke suggested. Maybe raise Angus beef. Maybe start a training center for aspiring young bull riders. And maybe he could raise his eyes and think about a young lady still far above him…

With hay to bale, he forced away his scattered thoughts and grabbed a quick lunch before heading out to the tractor. Before he could climb on to the machine, the enormity of this potential change drove him to his knees, and he at last gave vent to his tears.

"Lord, You have searched me and known me. You understand my thoughts from far off and are acquainted with all my ways. Who am I that You would give me such a gift of grace through no effort of my own? Give me wisdom each step of the way. No matter what Miss Petra says, I'll need to start paying her. You gotta…sorry, Lord. What I mean is, please let me win some good money at the rodeo so I can give her a healthy down payment. Thank You, thank You, Lord Jesus. Amen." Now, to dig in and make sure he was ready to ride.

June was getting used to Raeder being the last parent to pick up his child. In fact, she looked forward to it at the end of her teaching day. Each time he walked in the door, her heart did a little dance. He truly was a good friend and fun to be with. Now that she was RJ's teacher, she would get to see him even after their shared rodeo responsibilities came to an end. Today he looked particularly happy, and not just because RJ jumped into his arms and hugged his neck.

"Daddy, Miss June—I mean, Miss Mattson says me and you are going to 4-H tonight, and I finally get to be a Cloverbud."

"She did?" Raeder sent her a warm, full-face smile, and his voice held a note of laughter. "That's right. I almost forgot. We better get home and eat supper, then. Thanks for the reminder, June."

"You're welcome. I'm so glad they finally got qualified volunteers for the Cloverbuds. At least half of my class will be joining tonight, and I'm part of the welcoming committee." For some reason she didn't understand, she didn't want him to leave. But what could she say to keep him here when the entire school was being dismissed?

"I got an idea." His grin hadn't left his face since he stepped into the room. "How about we grab a bite to eat together before we go to the meeting. That is, if you don't have supper plans."

Had he read her mind? "No plans. I'd love to." She gathered her students' papers and shoved them into her satchel. "I have to run by my house and change clothes. That okay?"

"No problem. Let's go."

At home, while Raeder and RJ waited in his Bronco, she dashed inside to don jeans, a green polo shirt with the stampede logo, a green blazer and brown boots. She tucked her queen sash into her hatbox along with her hat and hurried back out.

"Wow, you look mighty fine, Miss Riverton Stampede." Raeder still hadn't stopped smiling.

"Thanks." She gave him a sidelong glance. "You seem mighty pleased about something. Out with it."

His laugh was the most carefree she'd ever heard from him. "Miss Petra and Zeke Baldwin got married today at the courthouse."

"What!" She squealed. "Oh, my hot tamales! That's so amazing…and wonderful!"

"Ugh!" RJ piped up from the back seat. "I don't like hot tamales."

Which sent both June and Raeder into fits of laughter.

"Yeah, Miss Petra asked me to give her away." His voice softened. "Said I was like a son to her."

"Awww. That's so sweet." June's eyes filled and she blotted away the tears before they could ruin her makeup. From his expression, she could see he was trying to hide his own feelings. "I sense there's something more. Spill it."

He glanced in the rearview mirror. "I meant to tell Peanut first, but I don't mind including you with the news. Miss Petra wants me to buy her ranch, and I said yes."

For a moment, June couldn't speak. "Oh, Raeder, how wonderful. This is what you've always wanted, right?"

"Yep." He shot her a grin. "The Lord works in mysterious ways. If I hadn't been laid up last year, I would have moved on to the next rodeo and missed out on, well, lots of things. Good things sure can come from bad."

"And now, you don't have to ride in the rodeo." She wanted to add "because you no longer have anything to prove to your father," but didn't. However, she could hope and pray!

"Where'd you get that idea?"

"Daddy, is Miss Petra gonna move away?" RJ's voice held a plaintive note.

"Yes, she is, Peanut, but we can see her anytime we

want to." Raeder's brow furrowed, as he whispered to June. "I didn't think about him missing her."

She was still back at his question—where had she come up with the idea he wouldn't ride again? Now she came up with a question of her own. Who would take care of RJ when Raeder was busy with dangerous parts of his ranch work? The poor little guy had endured a lot of big changes in his short five years.

They parked at a diner near the stampede arena, settled into a booth and ordered the special, liver and onions, much to RJ's disgust. "I want a hot dog."

As they waited for their food, June had her own good news to share. "FYI, Cousin Rob texted me that the banner company in Santa Fe is able to expedite our order for all of our sponsors as well as a new one for the stampede."

"Wow, looks like everything's coming together." He stared out the window beside their booth. "Y'know, I might have an idea for the band."

"Great. What is it?"

"My sibs used to play at events near home when they were in high school."

She watched the struggle on his face. "And you haven't called them because…?"

He exhaled long and slow. "It's been a long time since I've talked to anybody up there. I don't have any idea what they're doing."

"You still have their numbers?"

He pulled his phone from his hip pocket and tapped it. "Yeah. At least, what they were four years ago."

"And you're going to try one of them now, right?" She gave him a teasing grin. "Who are…were you closest to?"

"My sister Ally." Again his brow furrowed. "I…"

"Two orders of liver and onions." Their server brought

steaming plates of food. "And a hot dog for the young cowboy." She winked at RJ. "Anything else?"

"A refill of my sweet tea, please." June pointed to her glass. After the woman left, she focused on Raeder again. "Would you bless the food?" She was already blessed to learn he liked liver and onions. It was hard to find someone who shared her quirky tastes.

He said a brief prayer, his voice sounding a little strained. After "Amen," he said, "Let's eat it while it's hot."

"Ahem. That phone call?"

"I promise I'll do it later." He cut RJ's hot dog in half, then dug into his own food.

She loved watching him take care of his precious son. Most men she knew left such small caring acts, and even bigger ones, to their wives. She sensed he was a man who would cut the hot dog even if he had a wife to do it. She would love to know what he'd been taught that instilled such care for others in him. If he contacted his family in Wyoming about their band, maybe he could reconnect with them in other ways. Wouldn't they want to know about his buying a ranch? Wouldn't he want to know if his sisters or brothers had married? Had kids? To be honest with herself, she wanted to know all about the Westfall family, who lived so far away and, despite his issues with his father, had gone into making Raeder such a good man. A man she couldn't deny that she cared for a whole heap.

Following the 4-H meeting, Raeder drove June back to the church to pick up her truck. After the emotional high of the morning and the fun of enrolling Peanut in the Cloverbuds program, where he learned about showing his chickens, June's pesky reminder that he promised to call his family brought him back down to earth. But a promise was a promise.

He followed June and saw her safely inside her house, then drove home. With a sleepy Peanut settled in bed, thumb in mouth, Ralph the giraffe tucked in his arm, in their strangely quiet house, he sat in the living room and stared at his phone like he didn't know how to use it.

At last, he tapped Ally's number…and prayed she wouldn't answer.

"Raeder!" He recognized that squeal even after all this time. "Ma, it's Raeder."

Oh, no. She was at home. Who else was there?

"Raeder, talk to me," Ally ordered, with a hint of pleading. "I'm putting you on Speaker. It's just me and Ma here right now."

His heart turned to mush. "Hey, sis. What's happening?"

"What do you mean 'what's happening'? You're the happy wanderer in this family. What's happening with you?"

Happy wanderer? Was that how they thought of him?

"Honey, don't scold him." Ma's voice.

Raeder swallowed the emotion trying to claim him. "Hey, Ma. Love you." The words came out without thought, and now he could hear Ma crying. "Maybe this is a bad time."

"Don't you dare hang up." Ally had always been bossy. "Why'd you call?"

"Is Peanut okay?" Ma asked.

Her question broke his restraint. Not hearing any other voices on their end, he launched into a brief summation of his life for the past four years, except for the bull-riding disaster. In return, he learned Ally was engaged to a boy Raeder vaguely remembered from high school, and along with their two brothers and Giselle, they were still playing for local events around Douglas.

"We've played at banquets for groups like Kiwanis, and

last week, we got an invitation to play at a fair in Cheyenne next month."

At that, Raeder remembered why he'd called. "Wow, that sounds great, sis. You must be real good. Say, maybe you could help me out. Like I mentioned, I'm working with the committee for our rodeo that's coming up in a week and a half. We lost our band for the kickoff dinner and the dances the next two nights. Turns out they got an urgent call from a Nashville recording studio, so we need a replacement and quick. If you aren't booked, can you drive down and play for us those three days? We can put you up, and the pay is pretty good." He gave her the details, and she said she'd get back to him the next day. With that settled, she and Ma updated him on Colin, Giselle and Elliott. They talked late into the night until his phone battery signaled it was about out of juice.

"I'll look forward to your call, sis. 'Bye, Ma."

"'Bye, son." The catch in Ma's voice touched Raeder to his core. Why had he waited so long to call? And how could he make it up to her for his neglect? The only subject they hadn't spoken about was Pa. He tried not to care how the old man was doing, but oddly, he did.

As if Pastor Tim had been privy to Raeder's thoughts, the Sunday morning sermon gave him some helpful insight. "We don't choose the family we're born into. Sometimes a person is blessed with godly parents who fill the home with love and acceptance. Others face a more difficult path. Perhaps a parent makes wrong choices, perhaps wounded by their own upbringing. Perhaps we make our own mistakes that spoil the family dynamic. Whatever has happened, God has a family plan that can help and heal. If you know Jesus Christ as your Savior, Romans 8:14 encourages us with this truth—'those who are led by the Spirit of God are the children of God,' and as His children, 'we are God's heirs.' No matter what dysfunctions exist in our earthly family, God has changed our spiritual heritage. We are adopted into His family. Most amazing of all, God invites us to call Him *Abba*, Father, and as I've said many times, Abba translates as Daddy, the tenderest way by which we are encouraged to address Him."

"You're my daddy." Seated beside Raeder, Peanut whispered a little too loudly, and several folks behind them chuckled. "Can God be my daddy, too?"

Raeder's emotions had gotten out of hand far too much lately, but Peanut's innocent question caused those emotions to well up almost beyond his control. He put a finger to his lips. "Shh."

"But can He?" The whisper was softer and punctuated with a hint of worry.

Sensing Peanut's question was deeply important to him, Raeder settled for answering with a smile and a nod, which seemed to satisfy him. He leaned against Raeder's arm and stuck his thumb in his mouth. Love for his son welled up in Raeder's heart. There wasn't anything he wouldn't do for him.

While they were still in high school, Audra had shown him a verse in the book of Ephesians that said God had accepted him in His beloved Son. Accepted! After a lifetime of being rejected by his own pa, who'd probably never known such acceptance. That truth had turned his life around. And now, when it came to fathers and sons, Raeder wanted to follow God's example, not Pa's, loving and accepting Peanut without reservation, and of course being there and providing for him.

Did that mean giving up bull riding, as he knew June was praying he would? But if God had given His only Son for him, maybe He was calling Raeder to give up the sport he loved so much so he could be there for Peanut. He'd have to think on that a bit more…

Now, as Pastor Tim gave the usual invitation for anyone wanting to accept Christ to come forward and pray with him, Raeder finally understood his father. Pa was a broken, bitter man who needed Jesus, plain and simple. That was way more important than Raeder getting his approval. Pa probably didn't even accept or approve of himself.

A new kind of peace settled in Raeder's heart. From now on, along with praying for wisdom about his bull riding future, he'd pray for Pa's salvation.

Chapter Thirteen

"Welcome, everybody! Thank you for your support of our Riverton Stampede! Y'all havin' a good time?" Decked out in her queen regalia, June stood on the stage in the conference-center reception hall at the stampede kickoff dinner. Behind her, Raeder's family band, Dusty Boots, had already warmed up the crowd of four hundred with some rousing music. His bragging about his sister Giselle's beautiful voice had been spot on, and she'd blessed them all with her traditional singing of the national anthem. Then Pastor Tim had prayed over the proceedings, including the fine dinner spread.

Along the sidewalls of the hall, long cloth-covered tables held barbecue beef, pork, chicken and all the trimmings, including a variety of desserts. Folks had paid at the door, then lined up to get their food before finding seats at the numerous tables that rimmed the space saved for dancing. Now they responded to her greeting with hearty Western whoops, cheers and whistles.

June lifted her hands to quiet them. "I know y'all are enjoying the food and the music." She glanced behind her at the five band members, four of whom were clearly Raeder's kin, with the same curly blond hair and brown eyes. "Let's give the Dusty Boots a round of applause."

More cheers and whistles followed.

"All right, now, y'all keep on eating while Everly Strait comes up here and tells you what's happening over the next two days." June walked to the side of the platform.

"Hold on a minute, June." Everly stepped up to the microphone.

She paused, always ready for whatever showboating he planned. He beckoned to her and she returned to center stage.

"Folks, I know y'all are proud of our pretty Miss Riverton Stampede." At the eruption of applause, he held up his hands to silence the crowd. "You'll see her opening the rodeo for the next two days, carrying the flag and cheering every event, plus competing in the barrel racing. What you don't know is that behind the scenes, Miss June has gone above and beyond those duties to make this year's event a success. She and our featured bull rider, Raeder Westfall…y'all remember Raeder. He had a bad fall at last year's stampede, but now, he's back to show us what bull riding's all about. Anyway, these two young people have traveled around making sure all the pieces are in place for a successful rodeo. They even booked this band." He gestured to the group behind him. "Raeder's own family band. Raeder, how come you ain't up here singing with 'em?" Not really wanting an answer, he went on. "So if you get a chance, you be sure to give a Riverton Stampede thank-you to Miss June Mattson and Mr. Raeder Westfall." He chuckled. "Okay, you can go now."

The crowd laughed as June walked back to the steps, where Raeder waited with a hand outstretched to help her down. Her heart kicked up. He'd been so proud to introduce her to his family, including his sweet mother, who'd come along with her kids. The committee had a table at the front, and they'd made a space for Mrs. Westfall and welcomed her like she'd come home. She sat there with RJ on her lap, loving every minute of being a grandma.

Everybody loved Raeder, and June had to admit she was pretty fond of him herself. Was *fond* the right word? Was it the excitement of the stampede and surrounding events that drew her to him to the exclusion of all the other cowboys who wanted to spend time with the rodeo queen? No, it was more than that. Since working with him on the committee, she'd grown as comfortable in his company as she was with most members of her own huge Mattson clan. They laughed at the same things, and he even liked liver and onions, the first person besides Mom who shared a fondness for that particular dish.

"Hungry?" Raeder seated her at the committee table, where a plateful of her favorites awaited, then sat beside her in front of his own food.

"You made a plate for me?" Again, her heart hitched. He was always so thoughtful.

"'Course. Miss Riverton Stampede shouldn't have to stand in line for her dinner." He smirked in his cute cowboy way. "Now, don't go gettin' barbecue sauce on your pretty white shirt."

"Ha." She loved bantering with him. "You just take care of your own shirt." A very nice hunter green Western-style shirt that enhanced his tanned complexion and brought out the sparkle in his brown eyes.

In the past ten days or so, since learning he could buy Miss Petra's ranch, he'd changed. Not for better or worse, just happier than she'd ever seen him. More self-confident. And even more the attentive gentleman in escorting her to the preliminary rodeo events. If he was just some random cowboy, his attentions would make her uncomfortable after a while. But this was Raeder, a man she'd grown to trust. The man she looked forward to seeing at the end of each school day when he picked up his adorable son. Frequently going to the diner for supper with him and RJ was as natural as sitting down with her own folks, almost like they were a family.

No, *fond* wasn't the right word, but was it love? She'd never really had a boyfriend, just some sweet crushes in high school, so she had no idea what true love was. Mom and Dad had always taught her and Eric that they shouldn't date just to be dating, but only to spend time with a person they could consider marrying. June's frequent times spent with Raeder had involved rodeo business, not dating. All that time, she'd resisted letting her feelings for him deepen because of his determination to risk his life by competing in bull riding.

She knew he planned to ride the bulls tomorrow and Sunday. Could she let go of her fears for him and pray he'd be finished with the sport after that? After all, he was in the process of buying his own ranch. Wasn't that his ultimate dream and the reason he'd entered the rodeo to begin with? Yes, she would pray for him—first, that he'd have safe rides these next two days, and second, that those would be his last rides forever. Then maybe she could let herself feel something more for him than fondness. With that settled, she turned her attention to Mrs. Westfall, eager to get acquainted with the lady who'd raised such an exceptional son and his talented siblings.

"Forget everything but your ride." Cody stood by the chutes with Raeder. The first day of competition had begun, and the bull riders were taking their turns now. "Get your feet under you. Mash him with your knees." He pointed to the next bull up, the one Raeder was about to ride. "Keep your center balanced and your weight on your legs, not on your backside. Take the fight to the bull and show him who's boss. Aim beyond eight seconds." Cody had been drumming these basics into Raeder for the past three months, even more so once they started training at Walt's ranch. And slowly but surely, Raeder's body had remembered what he'd known for years. He was ready.

"I got it, Cody." Raeder dragged his leather glove down his bucking strap, roughing its texture so it wouldn't slip from his hand or the bull. "This ain't my first rodeo."

Cody snorted. "You just had to say that, didn't you? I thought you were serious about this."

"I'll be serious when I ride ol' Spite and Malice tomorrow." He increased the pressure on his strap. Only Cody, Walt, Everly and Rob Mattson knew about his rematch with the undefeated bull. It was billed in the program as a surprise grudge match with the hope that more people would stick around clear to the end of tomorrow's rodeo. "Today's just another practice, but one I intend to win." He'd drawn a bull he'd ridden for eight seconds twice before. He knew all the ways it bucked and spun and twisted. His only concern was that the critter might not give him a wild enough ride to earn top points.

The rider ahead of him made it to the buzzer, the second one of the nine competitors in his event to do so. Walt's bulls must not be doing their job today.

Now it was his turn. He donned his helmet, handed his bucking strap to the men preparing his ride and watched them sling it around the animal's flank. Then he climbed over the chute's railing and, getting his feet under him, lowered himself onto the thrashing bull's back, which made the critter thrash some more. He gripped his strap in his left hand, gave the ride to Jesus, then gave a quick nod, signaling he was ready. The gate flung open, and bull number sixty-four bolted out into the arena, kicking for all it was worth. Raeder mashed it with his knees, kept his weight on his legs, twisted with the twists, turned into the turns, fought gravity and finally heard the buzzer sound over the crowd's wild cheering. He jumped free, landing on his feet, and dashed for the rails while the bullfighters and clown drew the bucking bull toward the alleyway. Satisfied he'd given it all he was worth—and so had the bull—he ripped off his helmet and waited to hear his score.

"That's a score of eighty-five for Raeder Westfall as he makes his comeback to bull riding! What a ride!" Rob shouted through the loudspeaker, while more cheers erupted from the stands. "Looks like he's over last year's bad fall. Way to go, cowboy!"

Raeder added his own "Whoop!" as he headed toward the locker room, his heart almost bursting. "Thank You, Jesus."

"Sis, you missed Raeder's ride." Eric sat in his wheelchair next to their folks in the VIP section of the stands. "You should have supported your boyfriend and watched him best that bull."

"He's not my boyfriend." June scowled at her brother, hoping he couldn't see through her denial. Raeder might not be her boyfriend, but he'd come to mean so much to her. She was glad Mom and Dad were chatting with the mayor and his wife, so they didn't hear Eric's comment and add their two cents.

"Oh, you mean you haven't had the DTR talk yet." He gave her a teasing grin.

She plopped down into the seat she'd abandoned twenty minutes ago when the bull riding had begun. Earlier in the program, she'd had a fairly good run at the barrels, but not a championship ride. Her lack of disappointment hinted that it might be time to let that part of her life go. "Eric, nobody says 'define the relationship' anymore."

"Don't change the subject. Raeder did a great job. You should support him."

"So you said." In truth, she felt only relief that he'd done so well. She'd always admired people with grit, and Raeder had it in abundance. If she truly cared about him, maybe she should step back and let him do what he had to do to bolster his self-respect. But if their relationship got more serious, was his continuing to ride something she could live with? She leaned close to her brother, her lifelong confidant. "I'm going to the dance with him this evening. Maybe it's time for that talk."

His teasing expression turned affectionate. "He's a good man. I'll be praying for you."

"Congratulations on your ride today." June looked up into Raeder's handsome face, happy to be in his arms for a slow dance in the conference hall later that evening.

"Did you watch?" His steady gaze held a world of meaning. Did he feel the need to define their relationship, too?

"You know I didn't. But I did pray."

"June…" He frowned and bit his lip. "Listen, I appreciate your concern. Your opinion is important to me." He gave her his adorable crooked grin. "*You* are important to me."

"That means a lot. You're important to me, too."

Now he grinned. "That's good to hear." The tenderness in his eyes melted her heart. "Look, I've been thinking about what you've been saying. I know I need to be around to take care of my son. And I want to be a better father than my pa, and that means giving up my own wants and needs. What would you think if I stop riding bulls after tomorrow?"

She gasped quietly. This was huge. "That would mean more to me than I can even say." Tears clouded her vision. "I understand why you have to do it. You need to win the prize money for a downpayment on Miss Petra's ranch. But just one more time, okay?" A tear slipped down her cheek. "Promise me?"

He gave her another sweet smile and sighed. "I promise." He grimaced comically. "And to surrender one more thing to your wise counsel, I've decided to start calling Peanut RJ."

She drew in a quick breath. "That's huge."

"Yeah, well, he likes when his classmates call him RJ, so I might as well let it go."

"You're such a good father." She leaned her head against his chest as the music continued. They hadn't really defined their relationship, but they were making serious progress toward something very special.

Raeder had planned to test the waters with June, planned to tell her that knowing her had changed his priorities. Made him a better father. Made him want to have with his family what she had with hers. Made him want to give up what had been his passion so he could please her because she was fast becoming his new priority. Maybe he even wanted to spend the rest of his life with her, but he'd hold on to that 'til later. At least she accepted his need to ride again tomorrow. No problem. He maybe should have told her about his grudge match with ol' Spite and Malice, but he'd let that be a surprise. He'd promised he wouldn't ride bulls again, and he wouldn't. But he'd also made a promise to Walt. Besides, riding that unrideable bull was something he had to do for his self-respect and to honor his word. Now he made a promise to himself. If everything worked out with June as he hoped, from now on he'd consult her about any promise he made to anybody about anything.

June knew better than to back out of the second day's barrel racing. Nobody had ever called her a quitter, and she wasn't about to become one now. "Finish what you start," her folks had always said…another reason she had to accept that Raeder needed to ride today as well. Oddly, as she and Sprinter waited in the alleyway, her competitive nature kicked in. If this was her last barrel race, she might as well go out a winner. Apparently, Sprinter had the same notion. True to his name, he sprinted into the arena and took the three barrels like a whirlwind, dashing back to the finish line in what felt like their fastest time ever. She heard the roar of the crowd in the stadium.

"Twelve point nine seconds!" Cousin Rob practically shouted into the microphone. "A new stampede record! Ladies and gentlemen, give it up for our Miss Riverton Stampede." The crowd roared their approval again.

Her pulse racing as fast as Sprinter's run, she worked hard to catch her breath, at last calming enough to watch the next competitor. At the end of the event, with scores combined for the two days, June came in second and won a silver buckle and a hefty cash prize. She would use it to buy supplies for her students whose parents struggled to keep them in the private school. She hurried to the locker room and changed back into her dressy queen outfit. Today, she would grit her teeth and watch Raeder take his last ride.

She settled into her seat in the stands next to Eric's wheelchair. At the reminder of his loss, she felt a twinge of fear for Raeder. He'd drawn a different bull today, one that, according to Eric, had made short work of its riders the day before. But all the bulls fought hard to throw their riders, just as all the riders fought hard to stay on.

"Lord, give him a safe ride."

Eric gripped her hand. "Lord, give him a winning ride."

"Okay. I can 'amen' that. A winning ride is a safe ride."

"You're getting the picture, sis."

Before she could shoot back a teasing response, Raeder and bull number thirty-seven broke from the chute, fighting for all they were worth. Without thinking, June jumped to her feet.

"Ride 'em, Raeder! Hang on. You got this. Go, go, go!"

The crowd screamed their encouragement for the seemingly endless eight seconds. At the blast of the horn, Raeder jumped free. He was safe! He was done with bull riding! And June's heart was bursting with happiness…and love?

At the end of the event, his score of eighty-three combined with his previous day's points earned Raeder the top prize of 64,000 dollars. June didn't know the particulars of his arrangements with Miss Petra, but surely that would be a sufficient down payment so he could call the ranch his own. And if things between them progressed as she hoped, she'd be pleased to one day make it hers as well.

She settled back into her seat, curious to find out what the surprise grudge match was that would come up after the next round of steer wrestling. If she knew Everly and Cousin Rob, it was probably some made-up shenanigans between the rodeo clown and the tame steer he used to give the audience a laugh between events.

After the steer wrestling, Cousin Rob put on his serious voice. "All right, folks. You've been waiting long enough. First, here's a little background. Last year, our brand-new champion bull rider, Raeder Westfall, rode a bull called Spite and Malice, a name that critter deserves more than any other. That bull has never been ridden for a full eight seconds."

June sat up, a sick feeling rising in her chest. She glanced at Eric, who lifted his hands and shrugged. Mom and Dad shook their heads, clearly in the dark, too.

"So Spite and Malice not only tossed our hero off, he also

trampled on him real bad. Took surgery and a long recovery for ol' Raeder to make his comeback. But, folks, as you've already seen, Raeder is back to prove to that bull that you can't keep a good man down."

The crowd burst into cheers again.

"Focus on chute number four," Rob said, "'cause you're about to watch the grudge match of the century."

Heart clenching and breath stalled in her chest, June jumped up and turned toward the stairs.

Eric grabbed her hand. "C'mon, sis…"

Before he could finish, the clang of the chute gate sounded. She pulled her hand away and bolted up the steps, refusing to watch. If she didn't have queen duties in the closing ceremonies and tonight at the dance, she would keep running, all the way out of the stadium.

Raeder had broken his promise not to ride the bulls after today's competition, and she would never trust him again.

Every muscle, every instinct, screamed out that surely eight seconds had passed. Yet Raeder heard no horn and the bull continued to buck, twist, kick and jump, treating its unwanted burden like a ragdoll to dispose of as violently as possible. But Raeder would not let go.

Mash his knees. Use his legs. Anticipate the next twist. Right hand in the air. Stay upright. He could do this. *Would* do this.

After a seeming eternity, the cherished sound of the horn blast reached his brain, along with the roar of the onlookers. He'd done it! Now, to dismount. But the bull had no intention of letting him down easy. As though comprehending it had finally been bested, it threw up its back legs, twisted and dropped down on its front knees. Raeder's teeth jarred despite his mouth guard, and he plunged headfirst between the bull's horns, feeling the lift of his legs as the bull came up, tossing him heels over head, where he slammed into the dirt. And his world went black.

Chapter Fourteen

Behind the stands, June could hear the blast of the horn signaling eight seconds, then the roar of the crowd signaling the rider had made it all the way. But suddenly there was silence. Her heart seemed to stop. A rodeo audience only went quiet when disaster happened and someone was badly injured. She tried to force her feet to move, but fear froze her in place. Then another roar rose up, along with wild cheers and whistles. Which could only mean he was okay. As relief replaced fear, June came close to falling to her knees. Then anger replaced relief and stiffened her spine. She would never forgive him for giving her such a fright, but most important, for breaking his promise.

Somehow, she managed to complete her duties, in particular sticking around in the arena lobby for an hour to sign her queen pictures for fans, especially the little girls who wanted to follow in her footsteps. She even managed to make it to the closing dance, where Dusty Boots played, reminding her of better times and the man about whom she'd been so mistaken.

As if summoned by her thoughts, Raeder ambled up to her looking none the worse for whatever had happened in the arena five hours ago.

"Miss Riverton Stampede, may I have the next dance?"

Smiling, he held out his hand as if everything was all right between them.

Always mindful of her public image, she returned her queen smile, the one that said "friendly but unavailable." "Sorry, cowboy. I only dance with people whose word I can trust." She turned away, ignoring the bewilderment on his face. Did he truly not know what he'd done?

The rodeo had ended, and along with it, June's forced proximity to Raeder. She'd refused to answer his numerous attempts to reach her by phone, so now, she had only to face morning drop-off at school that day. With other parents to greet, she had no trouble ignoring Raeder. Later that afternoon, at the end of class, she busied herself with Janice Ortman and her twins, who'd volunteered to stay and help her cut out some figures for tomorrow's lesson.

"Miss June, I mean, Miss Mattson…" She looked up to see RJ gazing at her with a trust and affection beaming from his brown eyes that broke her heart. "Are you going to supper with Daddy and me?"

Raeder stood in the doorway watching. "Liver and onions at the diner?" His hopeful expression almost did her in.

"Nope. Sorry. Busy tonight." She turned a shoulder to avoid his stare. "Your girls are doing so well, Janice." She launched into a description of the twins' particular talents. To her relief, she heard the door close. A glance told her he'd left.

The next morning, when he didn't stay by the door as RJ walked to his desk, a pinch of disappointment struck her, until she shook off her foolishness. He'd clearly gotten the message and wouldn't bother her anymore.

But if that was what she truly wanted, why was she so depressed?

* * *

Saturday afternoon, with next week's lessons prepared and nothing good on television, June plopped down on the living room couch and pulled out the knitting she'd abandoned last winter when she started preparing for the Miss Riverton Stampede competition. Beside her, her cat Muffin pawed at the ball of yarn.

"Hey, sis." Eric rolled into the room and parked his wheelchair facing her. "What do you hear from Raeder? Has he recovered from conquering that bull?"

"You know, you can be so annoying." Determined not to look up, she kept her eyes on the brown-and-orange project in her hands. "You know very well I'm not speaking to him after he broke his promise not to ride again."

"Uh-huh."

Undoing stitches where she'd purled instead of knitted by mistake, she could feel his big-brother stare and finally raised her eyes to face him. "What?"

"Why are you mad at Raeder for keeping his promise to Walt?"

"That's even worse. After we went out to Walt's to persuade him to provide the rodeo stock, he never told me about that promise. If Dad hadn't been talking to Walt and accidentally learned about their agreement, I'd never have known. Raeder let me believe Walt was doing us a favor because I went there as Miss Riverton Stampede." In truth, it was her own vanity that made her think that. She hadn't even been on the porch when Raeder and Walt made their deal. She'd only seen the handshake and assumed she was the cause of Walt's change of mind. "Besides, I just can't let myself care for or love a man who thinks nothing of risking his life." She forbade herself to look at the legs her brother would never stand on again.

But he did. And then he looked at her. "Listen, kid—you've been around rodeo all your life. It's a dangerous occupation for all its participants, not just bull riders. I knew the risk I was taking when I competed. But I would do it again in a heartbeat if I could."

Her eyes burned with unshed tears as he repeated what he'd often said.

"Admit it," he continued. "Every time you get on a horse or get in a car or drive an ATV around this ranch, you could have a freak accident. Stuff happens. But we have to live our lives without being scared. What's that verse? 'What time I am afraid, I will trust in thee.' We do what we're called to do and trust the Lord."

This was getting dangerous to her heart. "Sermon over?"

"Nope." He chuckled. "What are you really afraid of? Loving a man who might get injured while doing something he's passionate about?" He smirked. "Or are you afraid of loving, period?"

"Muffin, stop. You're tangling my yarn." As she nudged the cat away, she couldn't even remember what she'd been making all those months ago. A sweater? A scarf? An afghan?

He reached over and set a hand on hers. "Take a chance on Raeder. You know he's a good man, so you don't have anything to be afraid of." He turned his chair and rolled toward the door. "Now the sermon's over."

As his words sank into her mind and heart, she knew he was right. All the things she'd learned about Raeder over these past months added up to make an exceptional man, one she'd tried not to fall in love with for the flimsiest of reasons, but failed. She did love him, so it was time to make things right with him. She put aside her knitting, grabbed her keys and dashed out to her truck, praying all the way he would forgive her for being so…unforgiving.

Seated at the kitchen table, Raeder stared at his phone, studying the figures in his bank account. Should he make the down payment to Miss Petra for the ranch or pack up Peanut and go back to Wyoming with his family?

"Penny for your thoughts." Ma had stayed behind for a visit when his sibs had headed back home for another gig. Over this past week, they'd restored the close relationship they'd had while he was growing up, so it had been a comfort to have her here and a pure joy to watch her interact with Peanut. He'd already poured out his heart over losing June. It hurt that she'd seemed to care about him yet hadn't bothered to check on him after he got the wind knocked out of him by ol' Spite and Malice. Parts of him still ached from the fall.

"Aw, you know. Same thing." He set his phone down. The decision about the ranch would have to wait.

Ma poured herself a cup of coffee and sat adjacent to him. "Why don't you give it one more try?" She nodded toward the phone. "Or better still, go see her. Maybe without the distractions of other people around, she'll be willing to talk with you."

"I don't know, Ma. I really blew it when I didn't set her straight about riding that bull or the deal I'd made with Walt. I didn't mean to mislead her, but…"

"But you can see how it looked to her." She poked his side. "Go on. I'll watch RJ. Gotta help him make that new Lego project."

He felt a little blip in his chest, the kind that hinted at something good. After all, Ma's advice had never steered him wrong. "Okay. I'll do that." He drained his coffee cup and stood. "Let me tell Peanut… RJ." He was getting used to that name for his son, and Ma liked it a whole bunch.

After promising RJ he'd bring home ice cream, he drove toward Eli Mattson's ranch on the other side of town. Should he stop for flowers? Maybe chocolates? He didn't even know what kind June liked. Before he could settle the question, he saw a familiar red pickup headed his way. June! He came screeching to a stop right there on the highway. When she did the same, he did a U-turn and pulled up behind her on the shoulder.

June hopped out of her truck and came running, so he got out and opened his arms wide, hoping for all he was worth that she meant what he hoped she meant. Sure enough, she did. She jumped into his arms like a pouncing cat, nearly knocking him over. He hugged her tight and swung her around like he'd seen sweethearts do on television.

"Oh, Raeder, I'm so sorry—"

"June, honey, can you ever forgive me?"

They spoke at the same time, then laughed. Then hugged some more. Raeder leaned back and brushed a hand across her cheek.

"Darlin', I should have told you Walt only agreed to let the stampede use his stock if I had that grudge match with ol' Spite and Malice." He grimaced. "I knew how you felt about my bull riding, but I was only thinking about myself… how I could prove myself."

"Oh, Raeder, I should have tried harder to understand what that ride meant to you instead of only seeing the danger." She sniffed back tears, then laughed softly. "I know you needed to prove yourself *to* yourself, to 'get back on the horse,' as the old saying goes. But I cared too much…" She stopped and tucked her lower lip between her teeth.

Raeder's heart leaped sky-high. "Um, are you saying what I think you're saying? Like…maybe you love me?"

Her cheeks flushed. "Maybe…" A cute little grin appeared on her pretty pink lips.

"Well, let me help you out. I've had a crush on you since I first saw you teaching Peanut in Sunday school. The more I got to know you, that crush's grown into l-love." He cleared his throat. "I love you, June."

Her eyes shone with fresh tears. Why did women always cry about these things?

"Oh, Raeder, I love you, too. I truly, dearly love you."

He pulled her into another hug, and she gave back as good as she got.

After a few minutes, he said, "Sweetheart, I should talk to your pa, your dad, first, but would you mind if I ask his permission to propose to you?"

"Oh, Raeder, that would make me the happiest woman in the world."

At that, he had to hug her again. And just for good measure, he kissed her right then and there, barely noticing the many vehicles passing by and blowing their horns. Were those friends glad to see them make up? Or just strangers who liked to see a cowboy win his lady?

Unlike many of her girlfriends and female Mattson cousins, June hadn't spent a lot of time thinking about a future wedding. Or about a husband, for that matter. She always figured the Lord would provide both at the right time. Now that she had her cowboy and would have her degree in a few months, wedding plans needed to come together pretty fast. She would have been happy to marry at the courthouse like Miss Petra and Zeke, but for some reason, Raeder wanted a little more. She gave up and decided to show him what a Mattson wedding was all about, an event even grander than Sam and Juliet's.

After much discussion, she and Raeder settled on their

wedding party. Her matron of honor would be Juliet. His best man would be Sam. Two of her six bridesmaids would be Raeder's sisters, and the other four, Mattson girl cousins. His two brothers would be groomsmen, with Mattson boy cousins, including Eric, wheelchair and all, to fill in the rest. RJ would, of course, be ring bearer, and Sam and Juliet's daughter, Sassy, would once again be flower girl, even though she was getting a little tall for that job.

Spring semester sped past, with June loving what she learned in her evening and online education classes. After graduation, she'd need more continuing education credits to qualify for her permanent teaching certificate, but that could come in the fall. Graduation came and went with Raeder cheering her on while he kept his ranch going by day and spruced up the soon-to-be-their-own ranch house in the evenings.

In May, June crowned the new Miss Riverton Stampede, happy to have served and happier to set aside the title. Then, on the first Saturday in June, she followed her bridesmaids down the center aisle of Riverton Community Church on Dad's arm to meet Raeder at the altar. She couldn't tell who was happier, Raeder or her, because her eyes were too full of happy tears.

Raeder had gotten pretty good at figuring out who most of the Mattson clan were, but at the wedding reception, he kept meeting more. June told him if somebody addressed him as "Cousin Raeder," that was a signal he or she was kin. It felt good to be part of such a loving, accepting family. June's folks had been more than kind, never once hinting at any difference in their social status. They only wanted their kids to be happy, and that now included Raeder. The day before the wedding they'd driven out to his ranch, hauling their horse trailer. Eli unloaded Shadow and all his tack, saying he didn't have time to give the stallion any attention and maybe Raeder could use him to start his own horse farm. With that kind of welcome into the Mattson family, Raeder knew he truly was one of them.

His own family had shown up for the wedding, with his sibs offering a harmonious rendition of the "Lord's Prayer" during the ceremony and playing a couple of bluegrass numbers at the reception. Ma had beamed her approval of all the proceedings. Even Pa showed up at the last minute to sit beside Ma, but after the ceremony he hadn't approached Raeder in the crowd of several hundred in the fellowship hall.

"You have to speak to him." June looped her arm around Raeder's. "I'll go with you. No matter what he says, if he tries to put you down, remember all you've accomplished." She gave him her saucy grin. "Go face him like you faced that stupid bull."

He chuckled. "Can't I just ride ol' Spite and Malice again, instead?"

"Ha! Never, never again."

"Yes, ma'am." He didn't mind doing whatever pleased his beautiful bride. She had become his priority and making her happy had become his new passion. "Awright, let's go."

Arm in arm, they wended their way through the crowd, stopping every few feet to received congrats and best wishes. Looking lost and bewildered, Pa was standing off to the side by himself, and for the first time ever, Raeder felt sorry for him.

Raeder stuck out his hand. "Hey, Pa. I'm glad you came. This is my new bride, June Mattson, er, Westfall."

Pa stared at Raeder's hand like it was a rattlesnake but finally took it. Weakly at first, then he grasped it firmly. "You got yourself a winner, boy." He nodded to June. "How'd you manage that?"

She didn't give Raeder a chance to answer. "Pleased to

meet you, Mr. Westfall. I sure did have a hard time lassoing this cowboy. He's everything I ever looked for in a husband. I know you're proud of him for all his accomplishments."

Pa blinked like she was talking in a foreign language, then finally mumbled, "Uh, sure."

"Now, you'll excuse us, won't you?" She gave him her queen smile. "We got lots more people to thank for coming out to celebrate our wedding."

"Yes, ma'am." A shy grin appeared. "Congratulations."

As they walked away, Raeder squeezed her arm tighter. "How'd you do that?"

"Well, we've been praying for him to come to Jesus, and you catch a lot more flies with honey than with vinegar."

He stopped and tugged her around in front of him. "I'm so blessed to be married to the sweetest honey of all." And he planted a kiss on her sweet lips right there in front of everybody.

Somewhere around them, somebody started clapping, and it seemed to Raeder everybody in the room joined in. And maybe, just maybe, up in heaven, Audra was applauding, too, at seeing her cowboy win his very own rodeo queen.

* * * * *

If you enjoyed this book, pick up these connected titles by Louise M. Gouge about other members of the Mattson family:

Safe Haven Ranch
A Faithful Guardian
Feuding with the Cowboy

Available now from Love Inspired!

Dear Reader,

Thank you for choosing *The Cowboy's Last Rodeo*. I hope you enjoyed reading the love story of Raeder Westfall and June Mattson, who live along the Rio Grande in my fictional town of Riverton, New Mexico.

This book is a legacy sequel to my Love Inspired Historical novella, *Yuletide Reunion*, published in the anthology *A Western Christmas* (2015), two LIH novels, *Finding Her Frontier Family* (2022) and *Finding Her Frontier Home* (2023), and my contemporary Love Inspired books, *Safe Haven Ranch* (2024), *A Faithful Guardian* (2024) and *Feuding with the Cowboy* (2025).

When I began writing these contemporary stories, I needed a name for a pre-K Sunday school teacher for my hero's nephew in *Safe Haven Ranch*, so I chose June because when I was about six years old, my sixteen-year-old Sunday school teacher, June Reynolds, led me to faith in Jesus Christ in a little community church in Theodore, Alabama. That was long ago and far away, and I look forward to seeing the real-life June in Heaven one day. As my series progressed, I wanted my fictional rodeo queen June to have her own love story. Who better for her to fall in love with than a rodeo champion? Along comes single dad Raeder Westfall, whose darling little boy just might need a new mama. Fun fact: I've been waiting many years to name a character Raeder—pronounced *Ray-der*—in honor of a college classmate who went on to become an opera singer, not a cowboy.

I love to hear from my readers, so if you enjoyed *The Cowboy's Last Rodeo*, please write and let me know. Please also

visit my website: louisemgougeauthor.blogspot.com, find me
on Facebook: facebook.com/LouiseMGougeAuthor or follow me on BookBub: bookbub.com/profile/louise-m-gouge.

God bless you.

Louise M. Gouge

Get up to 4 Free Books!

We'll send you 2 free books from each series you try
PLUS a free Mystery Gift.

Both the **Love Inspired**® and **Love Inspired**® **Suspense** series feature compelling novels filled with inspirational romance, faith, forgiveness and hope.

YES! Please send me 2 FREE novels from the Love Inspired or Love Inspired Suspense series and my FREE gift (gift is worth about $10 retail). I may cancel anytime by emailing ReaderServiceInfo@Harlequin.com or by calling 1-800-873-8635. If I don't cancel, I will receive 6 brand-new Love Inspired Larger-Print books or Love Inspired Suspense Larger-Print books every month and be billed just $7.19 each in the U.S. or $7.99 each in Canada. That is a savings of 20% off the cover price. It's quite a bargain! Shipping and handling is just 75¢ per book in the U.S. and $1.75 per book in Canada.* I understand that accepting the free books and gift places me under no obligation to buy anything—they are mine to keep for free no matter what I decide.

Choose one:

☐ **Love Inspired Larger-Print**
(122/322 BPA G3CD)

☐ **Love Inspired Suspense Larger-Print**
(107/307 BPA G3CD)

☐ **Or Try Both!**
(122/322 & 107/307 BPA G3CE)

Name (please print)

Address   Apt. #

City   State/Province   Zip/Postal Code

Email: Please check this box ☐ if you would like to receive newsletters and promotional emails from Harlequin Enterprises ULC and its affiliates. You can unsubscribe anytime.

Mail to the **Harlequin Reader Service:**
IN U.S.A.: P.O. Box 1341, Buffalo, NY 14240-8531
IN CANADA: P.O. Box 603, Fort Erie, Ontario L2A 5X3

Want to explore our other series or interested in ebooks? Visit www.ReaderService.com or call 1-800-873-8635.

LIRLIS2603